THAT TIME IN SYDNEY

BOOK 6 OF THE WOLFGANG PIERCE SERIES

LOGAN RYLES

Copyright © 2021 by Logan Ryles. All rights reserved.

No part of this book may be reproduced in any form or by any electronic or mechanical means, including information storage and retrieval systems, without written permission from the publisher, except for the use of brief quotations in a book review.

THAT TIME IN SYDNEY is a work of fiction. Names, characters, places, and incidents either are the product of the author's imagination or are used fictitiously. Any resemblance to actual persons, living or dead, events, or locales is entirely coincidental.

ISBN: 978-1-7359031-7-0

Library of Congress Control Number: 2021911720

Published by Ryker Morgan Publishing.

ALSO BY LOGAN RYLES

THE WOLFGANG PIERCE SERIES

THE REED MONTGOMERY SERIES

Book 7: *Sundown*

THE PROSECUTION FORCE SERIES

Book 1: *Brink of War*

For Abby and Naomi

Thanks for keeping me inspired.

———

"Sydney is the city of fireworks."
— Baz Luhrmann

———

[1]

April, 2012

The jewelry shops in Manhattan were unlike any Wolfgang had ever seen, with plush black carpeting and lights that were dim enough to induce a tone of exclusivity but bright enough to bring every diamond beneath the glass counters to life in glittering glory. For six hours he wandered in and out of the shops, gliding down the cases with his hands in his pockets as he admired the massive stones encased in polished gold. From time to time, a salesman would approach, asking his name and offering a compliment about his coat, hair, or shoes.

It was the compliments that threw Wolfgang off. The friendliness by itself he might have accepted as genuine, but there was no way these austere men—

for some reason, they were all men—dressed in luxury suits with ties that cost more than Wolfgang's entire wardrobe, truly admired his cheap shoes or worn coat.

They were salesmen. What did he expect? They didn't know he carried sixty thousand dollars in cash in his pocket. It was the same song and dance as when he purchased a brand-new Mercedes SLK five months earlier. They hadn't taken him seriously then, either. And that was okay.

Wolfgang stopped in front of a case at the end of an aisle and stared down at a row of rings mounted on black velvet. Unlike the other cases that crowded the middle of the store, these rings featured smaller stones without the clutter of halos and multiple colors of gems. They were elegant. Simple in their beauty and style.

Like Megan.

A salesman with white hair combed neatly over his head appeared like a genie out of a bottle, smiling and drifting behind the counter. "Can I help you, sir?"

Wolfgang motioned to the case. "Can I see the one on the end?"

The man drew a cluster of keys from his pocket and unlocked the case, sliding the door back and reaching in with practiced elegance.

"I call it the Lady Jane," he said, giving the ring a

gentle dusting with a cloth before handing it to Wolfgang. "It's one of my favorites."

Wolfgang held the ring in his palm, fingering it. It was made of traditional yellow gold, split and woven near the top right before it met the diamond. The stone rested in a simple cradle by itself, beautifully cut in a traditional princess shape with no additional decoration or clutter.

"You said you call it the Lady Jane? That's not its name?"

The old man smiled. "It is. I named it."

"You made it?"

"I make all the rings in this case. Been making them for forty years."

"No kidding? This is your shop?"

The salesman beamed. "It is now. My father opened it not long after he emigrated from Italy. My son will take over when I die." He pointed to a younger man across the room who was speaking to a woman about a necklace. The man waved.

"That's remarkable," Wolfgang said. "I like the ring. Why do you call it that?"

"It's a play on words. Have you ever heard the term *plain Jane?*"

"Right. To describe something simple."

"Or ordinary. In today's world, everything has so much flash, so much glamour. Especially in New York. When my father opened this shop, it was a different world. Sometimes I think people have forgotten what true beauty is."

Wolfgang rolled the ring in his hand, examining it from different angles. He'd spent the whole afternoon browsing engagement rings priced as low as ten grand and as high as a hundred. Many were beautiful, but none of them had soul. None of them felt right.

He pictured himself holding Megan's hand, alone in someplace beautiful. He imagined dropping to one knee, his stomach fluttering as he recited the words he'd been rehearsing for weeks. Then he imagined drawing this ring from his pocket, holding it up to a setting sun, and whispering those four little words.

It was right. He felt it immediately. The simplicity and classic design were everything he saw in Megan.

"How much?"

The old man shrugged as if price were a random thing that changed by the minute and never really mattered. "I never make the same thing twice. Make me an offer."

"I don't know what it's worth," Wolfgang said. "I know nothing about jewelry."

The old man cocked his head. "How much is *she* worth?"

Wolfgang laughed. "That's a sly question if I ever heard one."

He laughed back. "Maybe, but not in the way you think."

Wolfgang laid the ring on the counter and pushed his hands back into his pockets. "She's worth . . . everything. More than I'll ever have."

The old man's smile deepened, becoming a little wistful and nostalgic. "Five grand," he said.

"Five grand? It's worth much more."

"I liked your answer. True love can't be faked."

Wolfgang reached into his pocket and withdrew ten thousand in hundreds. "Call this a tip, then. For fine craftsmanship."

"I appreciate it. I'll have my son get you a box."

Wolfgang picked up the ring again, staring into the stone and admiring the way the lights overhead reflected in the gem's heart, splitting into every color of the rainbow as he twisted the ring in his palm. He thought about Megan and the moment they shared at the top of Tokyo Tower six weeks earlier, when their feelings collided in a kaleidoscope of passion.

Megan was a member of Charlie Team, the elite espionage unit that Wolfgang worked for. From the moment they first met, he'd found her attractive, but that initial physical reaction had gradually shifted into a deeper passion that eventually became all-consuming. He'd pursued her and been denied repeatedly, running up against a wall that Megan refused to lower, even for somebody she admitted to liking.

But then came Tokyo—that night at the tower, followed by those hours spent exploring the city and getting drunk together, and ending with the hotel room overlooking downtown. It was unlike anything Wolfgang had ever imagined or dreamed of. It was life, and it was death. It was light, and it was dark. It was every side of his complex personality meshed with that of another, and it brought him joy he didn't think was possible.

After returning from Tokyo, his only fear had been that Megan didn't reciprocate his feelings, but he needn't have stressed. They spent every available moment together over the following weeks, bouncing between his apartment in St. Louis and her garden home in Minneapolis, exploring together, lying awake under starlit nights in the freezing cold of late winter, and taking long drives in the Mercedes. They talked about dreams and fears and what the future could be like.

And Wolfgang knew that no matter what the world brought him for the remaining years or decades of his life, he wanted to share it with her. So he sold the Mercedes, consolidated what cash he'd accumulated from his five missions with Charlie Team, and purchased fifteen acres in rural Upstate New York. Megan had talked about quitting the dangerous espionage work and living in the woods someplace quiet where she could pursue her dream of being a visual artist. Wolfgang would build her a home in those woods, close enough to Buffalo for him to look after Collins, his little sister. They'd quit the espionage life together, and then he'd figure out another way to keep the lights on.

They didn't need much. They didn't need fancy cars or private jets or a life full of adrenaline. Maybe Wolfgang would sell insurance or work in a factory building microwaves. He didn't really care. He just wanted more of the simple happiness he found with Megan.

Of course, Megan didn't know about these plans. She didn't know about the property in New York or the sold Mercedes or his plans to propose only weeks into their whirlwind romance. But he was no longer afraid of being bold.

Fortune favors the bold. Maybe love does, too.

Wolfgang accepted the box from the man's son and slipped the ring inside, then stepped back into the noise and bustle of Manhattan. He sucked in a deep breath of February air and gripped the box in his pocket, wondering how he would pop the question.

It was more than a question, of course, and it was more than a proposal of marriage. It was a proposal of a complete, dramatic shift in the trajectory of their entire lives. An offer of an alternate future.

Love favors the bold. God, let that be true.

Wolfgang looked up at the towers looming over him, casting long shadows over the streets as the sun began to set, and he decided he wouldn't worry about her response. He might not propose for another few weeks, or even a couple months. He'd wait until the moment was right.

Speaking of the moment . . .

Wolfgang checked his watch. It was a Rolex Submariner, presented to him by the director of SPIRE after Wolfgang rescued the director's daughter during a daring mission in Rio. Wolfgang had almost sold the watch during his pursuit of an average life, but he found enough cash for the land purchase without it, and he was glad. He wanted at least one memento of his life with Charlie Team.

It was 4:32, which meant it was time to head to the airport so he could get back to St. Louis and clean out his apartment. Wolfgang's phone buzzed, and he dug it out of his pocket. His stomach tightened at the prospect of Edric texting him about another mission, which was usually a welcome offer, but not today.

But the text was from Megan, and when he opened it, the first thing he saw was a picture. Megan stood in some kind of clothing store, one hand on her hip, with her head cocked to the side and a playful smirk on her lips. Her grey eyes shone as she draped a black bikini on a hanger over her body, as if she were testing it for size. The color contrasted her red hair perfectly, and Wolfgang's mind immediately generated an image of her wearing it. It was a damn good-looking image.

The phone beeped, and a message popped up beneath the picture.

IF ONLY WE WERE AT THE BEACH . . .

Wolfgang bit his lip, his plans to clean out his apartment a distant memory. He thought about the beach, long walks, sunsets, and proposals.

Why not?

He grinned and tapped out a quick reply, then held up his hand for a cab.

Wolfgang stood next to the window at Miami International Airport as flight 272 direct from Minneapolis touched down. His heart raced as he watched the sleek plane taxi toward the terminal, and he pictured Megan inside. It had been only four days since they were last together, but it felt like an eternity. He wondered if it would always be this way—if he would always count hours until he saw her again, and if they would always buy tickets to the beach at the drop of a hat because Megan found a swimsuit and the weather was nice.

He hoped so. Wolfgang had experienced enough loss and chaos to know that no life was a fairytale. But maybe the connection the two of them shared could be sheltered from the storm. Maybe he could keep the fire alive if he just sheltered it enough.

He rolled his shoulders and inspected himself, still unhappy with his ensemble. Megan had complained that he too often wore bland and boring clothes, so for the beach, he selected some pastel pink shorts and a Hawaiian shirt with enough flowers to qualify as a botanical garden. Flip-flops, Ray-Bans, and his Rolex completed the getup, but Wolfgang couldn't help feeling that he looked like a fool, and he kept glancing around the room to see if anybody was staring.

Who cares? If it makes her happy . . .

The plane docked to the terminal, and Wolfgang stood at arrivals, waiting for his first glimpse of her. Megan was so small, she looked like a teenager amid the crowd of bustling people pouring out of the tunnel, but he wouldn't have missed her in a football stadium. She wore a loose cotton blouse and capris, with her hair held back in a ponytail just the way it was when they first met.

Wolfgang raised a hand. "Megan!"

She spotted him, and confusion crossed her face. Then she broke out into a laugh. Megan shouldered her carry-on and hurried across the terminal, jumping into his arms with a little squeal. "Wolf!"

He wrapped her in a hug and spun once, then they kissed. Megan leaned in and held him, and for a moment, the airport simply vanished. He pulled her close and felt her tongue on his, and absolutely nothing else mattered.

Megan broke the kiss long before he would have and leaned back, holding his hands. She inspected his outfit and broke into another laugh. "What the *hell* are you wearing?"

Wolfgang scrunched his nose to drive his glasses back into place.

"You know . . . Beach clothes."

"Beach clothes? From the seventies?"

When Wolfgang flushed, she laughed and kissed him again, quickly this time. "I love it," she whispered.

They took a cab into the city, holding each other in the back seat and trying for a while to behave like adults. That effort evaporated within minutes, and Wolfgang forgot about the cab driver, convinced that lovers making out in his back seat was far from the worst thing he'd witnessed.

The cab ground to a halt in front of a hotel, but Wolfgang didn't notice until the driver politely cleared his throat.

"Forty-two fifty, sir," he said.

Wolfgang sat up and pushed his glasses into place, offering an apologetic grin. He pulled a hundred from his pocket. "Keep the change."

They piled out of the car, Wolfgang dragging the bag behind him.

Megan brushed her hair with one hand, then tilted her head back to inspect the building. "Where are we anyway?"

Wolfgang shrugged. "No idea. Someplace I found online."

"You got us a room?"

"I got us a suite."

"That sounds sexy."

"It will be when you get there."

She smacked his hand, and then they checked into the hotel.

The elevator was empty, and they found their way into each other's arms again, tangling in the corner for a moment before the bell dinged and a mom with two middle-school boys got on. Wolfgang and Megan retreated to the corner, nodding sheepishly. The mother scowled, but one boy shot Wolfgang an approving wink.

The room was as advertised—a beach-facing suite with a king-size bed, a minibar, and a massive jetted tub. Five months before, Wolfgang wouldn't have dreamed of taking Megan to a place like this, but now it felt like the most natural thing in the world.

Megan wandered to the window and looked out at the water. She smiled, and he thought it was a little sad. He wondered what memories brought that smile to her face, but decided not to ask. Some moments were better left in silence.

She turned back after a while and grinned. "So, what's on the agenda?"

Wolfgang collapsed on the couch and interlaced

his fingers behind his head. "Well, first, I'm gonna need to see you in that bikini. I mean, this whole trip was triggered by a suggestive photo. Gotta make sure you're beach-ready."

She laughed. "If by beach-ready, you mean whatever you're wearing . . . no. I'm afraid I'm not."

He grinned. "We'll figure it out."

"I'm sure. What else you got planned?"

"I'm thinking dinner. Some slow dancing to an island band. A long stroll on a quiet beach. A little poetry beneath the stars."

"Poetry?" She sauntered across the room and slid into his lap, running one arm behind his neck. He leaned in until their noses almost touched, but he didn't kiss her. He just wanted to savor the moment.

"You really know how to show a girl a good time."

"If you say so."

She pulled him close and kissed him, running her hands up his back. He pulled her in, and they twisted, falling onto the couch. Clothes hit the floor, and once again, the world faded away.

———

The night went pretty much according to Wolfgang's best-case scenario. He and Megan tumbled on the couch for half an hour, then found their way into the suite's giant shower. She dressed him in clothes she'd picked out for him—apparently Megan predicted his

poor wardrobe choice—and then she slipped a swimsuit cover over the bikini, refusing to let him see her
in it until they were on the beach.

They found their way to an ocean-side restaurant
with a live band and ate seafood until their stomachs
hurt. They danced on the open floor as the sun set,
and Wolfgang lost himself in Megan's laugh. He'd
never seen her so happy before or imagined that he
could feel this happy. He wound back through all the
speed bumps of his life, all the broken moments and
bitter losses, from his childhood in West Virginia to
his career as an espionage agent for hire. Nothing felt
like this. This was like the crescendo of a great
sonata. The moment when the stars align, the fireworks go off, and the world be damned. Life was
good.

As darkness closed over Miami Beach, they left
the restaurant and walked next to the water. It was
warm, and Megan tugged the swimsuit cover off. She
looked far better in the bikini than Wolfgang had
dreamed, and it was difficult to keep his eyes off her
as they danced in and out of the water, listening to
the waves wash over the sand as the distant island
music played in the background. There were hardly
any people, which Wolfgang thought was strange for
the time of year, but he found rapture in the quiet. It
was perfect.

A mile from the restaurant, they found a marina
full of million-dollar yachts, all resting at anchor on

the western side of the island. Only a chain barrier and a "Private Marina, Keep Out" sign blocked their path, and after a mischievous wink, Megan ducked beneath the chain and led Wolfgang down the pier, dancing over ropes and admiring the yachts. Each boat sat still in its slip, unmoved by the wind or the water, beautiful in its opulence.

Megan stopped at the end of the pier and faced downtown Miami, pulling Wolfgang close. He wrapped his arms around her, resting his chin on her shoulder as they both admired the downtown lights. Blues and greens, reds and yellows . . . the water was a light show with barely a ripple disturbing the perfect calm.

Megan let out a long breath. "Tell me something you've never told me."

"What do you mean?"

"I don't know . . . Tell me something you wouldn't tell anybody else."

He hesitated, watching the water glimmer beneath the skyline of the big city. The salt and the breeze were so perfect. So quiet.

"My name isn't Wolfgang."

"What?" She twisted her shoulders to look up at him.

He smiled. "It's something I wouldn't tell anyone else."

"What do you mean?"

"Just that . . . my name isn't Wolfgang. Or Pierce,

actually. When Edric found me in West Virginia, I needed a new start. I guess I thought a new name would help, so I told him to call me Wolfgang Pierce and . . . well, it stuck."

Megan cocked her head, a crooked, under-standing smile crossing her lips. "So, what's your real name?"

Wolfgang straightened and assumed his most austere, self-important expression. "Horace Artemus Hawthorn. The fourth."

Megan said nothing, then let out a nervous chuckle. "You're kidding, right?"

Wolfgang laughed. "Yeah."

"Oh, thank God. That's awful."

"My real name is Ricky. Or, Richard, really. Richard Ward."

He held his breath, waiting for a reaction. She said nothing—just stared a long moment with that same crooked smile on her face. "I love you, Ricky Ward."

"I love you, Megan Rudolph."

His heart pounded as he held her close and thought about the ring in his pocket. He'd taken it out of its box earlier that day so she wouldn't notice its bulk. Now it rode there, waiting for the perfect moment.

What moment could be more perfect than this?

Megan twisted to look at the city again, and Wolfgang wondered what to say. He'd spent weeks crafting the perfect speech, but now he couldn't remember a word of it.

Maybe he should just ask her. Just kneel and hold out the ring.

Wolfgang slipped his hand into his pocket, fingering the ring and thinking that he would just say what he felt. He'd tell her what he wanted and what he dreamed about. He'd tell her everything they could have together.

Footsteps tapped against the pier, jarring Wolfgang from his daydream. A tall man in jeans and an open black jacket walked toward them, his jaw set in a hard line.

"Here comes security," Wolfgang said.

Megan looked over her shoulder, flashing the man a disarming grin. "Are these boats for sale?"

The man said nothing, but walked faster. His hand dipped beneath his jacket, and Wolfgang's muscles tensed. The hand reappeared, clutching a gun with a suppressor affixed to its muzzle, and before Wolfgang could move or even shout, the man opened fire.

[3]

The muzzle of the gun twitched, and a familiar spitting sound ripped across the dock. Wolfgang's mind clicked into gear like a machine, taking over his confusion and denial and dominating him with a single thought: Protect Megan.

He slung himself sideways in front of her even as the first bullet scraped his ribcage, and the pistol popped again. Then the two of them went flying off the end of the pier, a tangle of arms and legs as the lights of Miami flashed by, and then the water closed over them.

Wolfgang's mind spun into overdrive, commanding him to reach the surface as his body consumed oxygen at an accelerated rate. But Megan's fingers closed around his wrist, pulling him downward, and he knew she was right. He kicked away from the surface into inky blackness, blind to everything except the pull of her hand on his. A few kicks farther, and then his free hand touched the slimy surface of a pier pylon, and he pulled himself beneath the dock.

His lungs burned, and the pounding in his chest reached his head, throbbing in a constant beat that promised the end of his life if he didn't find air. Megan's hand still clutched his wrist and held him down. He tugged on it, but she tugged back, pulling him farther into the blackness.

Wolfgang gritted his teeth and pushed away from the pier, following Megan. He couldn't see her, but the feel of tremors in the water helped him avoid her kicking feet as she pulled him deeper. Hard metal scraped his arm, and he turned to see the dark outline of a propeller only inches from his face. They were beneath one of the yachts, and panic blanketed his mind.

Breathe. I have to breathe.

He kicked harder, tracing Megan's arm up to her shoulder and pulling her close. They crossed beneath the bottom of the boat, still wrapped in darkness. Wolfgang's lungs felt ready to collapse, and his hands shook. Megan pulled up, and they both kicked for the surface.

Wolfgang's head broke through the saltwater like a submarine making an emergency blow. He sucked in air and thrashed to keep himself from sinking, dread overtaking his childhood swimming skills, and the only thing he could think about was making sure neither of them sank again.

"Megan?"

"Look out!" Megan called from behind him, and then she shoved him beneath the water at the same moment gunshots snapped from between the boats.

Again, the dark water closed overhead, but this time Wolfgang was ready for it. He kicked down deliberately, holding Megan's hand until his feet touched the sandy bottom. His natural buoyancy kept pulling him back toward the surface, but Wolfgang reached out and touched the barnacle-covered surface of a pylon and pulled close to it, holding the two of them against the bottom.

Megan reached out to him, her fingers touching his chest and then tracing up to his neck. She pulled him in until their noses were only an inch apart, and he caught the outline of her face. Then she held up a finger, right in front of his eyes.

Wolfgang nodded. He understood. He focused on counting seconds and ignoring the bursting sensation in his chest. It wasn't just his own life that depended on staying beneath the surface, it was Megan's. But if this was a waiting game, time was on the side of their would-be killer. Eventually they'd have to surface, and he'd be ready for them.

Wolfgang pointed upward, and Megan shook her head insistently, but Wolfgang held up a finger until she calmed, then pointed upward again, making a slow rising motion with his hand.

Up. Slowly.

Megan gave the thumbs-up, and Wolfgang let go of the pylon but didn't kick. They rose, inches at a time, remaining beneath the finger pier that shot out between two yachts. The water was about fifteen feet deep, and they didn't have far to go before breaking the surface, but they needed to do it quietly.

The last few feet felt like miles, and Wolfgang wondered what it felt like to lose consciousness. Would he just slip away? Would he know he'd pushed it too far?

His fingers broke the surface beneath the pier, and he grabbed the nearest board, bracing himself from making another dramatic surface. He eased their heads above the water an inch at a time, slowly contracting his arm until their noses broke the surface and they both sucked in precious oxygen. It was all he could do not to open his mouth and gasp like a water buffalo. Megan squeezed his hand, and he relaxed a little, sucking in another breath.

The underside of the pier was ten inches over his face—a row of thick planks with narrow cracks between them. The space between the planks and the water was black, broken only by streaks of light that cut in from the city. As he followed the pier back to its root, he saw the junction where this finger met with the primary pier. On either side of him, yachts rode at anchor, unmoving in the silent night.

Then he heard footsteps. They were distant—not on this finger and not on the main pier, either. The killer was someplace amid the yachts, checking one slip at a time.

Wolfgang turned to Megan and held a finger to his lips, then pointed toward the footsteps.

"We've got to get out of the water," he whispered. "We're sitting ducks."

"Are you hurt?" she asked.

It was only then that Wolfgang remembered the gunshot. He traced his fingers beneath the water to his ribcage and winced. A gash ran along his side, beneath his armpit. The best he could tell, the bullet had scraped him without ever actually entering his body, but when he withdrew his fingers, they were stained red.

Not great.

"I'll be fine. I want you to stay here. I'll get out and—"

"Are you crazy? I'm coming, too!"

Wolfgang started to object, but before he could, the thump of footsteps arrested his attention. Bright light shone from someplace beyond the yachts, and as Wolfgang looked out from beneath the edge of the pier, he saw its source.

The killer stood on the main pier, his gun in one hand and a flashlight in the other. He walked one board at a time, scanning the cracks between them and occasionally flashing the light over the dark water of each slip. There was no apparent pattern to his search, making it impossible to predict, but even a moron would know that it was only a matter of time before the light flashed across their faces.

"We've got to move," Wolfgang whispered.

The two pushed off the underside of the pier, sinking beneath the surface once more. This time, Wolfgang's heart didn't pound, and his lungs didn't burn. That would come, but for now, he was in control. He held Megan by one hand, and they swam towards the shore, diving beneath the belly of another yacht before rising underneath the next finger of the pier.

As Wolfgang cleared the water from his eyes, he saw the killer to his left, farther down the pier and moving away from him. The flashlight still shone at random beneath the pier and around the yachts, moving in increasingly erratic sweeps.

Wolfgang looked to the nearest yacht and noticed a swim ladder near the back. He thought momentarily about trying to hijack it, but it was a stupid idea. The keys wouldn't be in it, and even if they were, it would be much too slow.

"We should move to shore," Megan said, tugging on his arm. But again, Wolfgang did the math and knew they'd never make it. The pier was long, and they were a full fifty yards from the beach. If they hit the pier and ran, they would never make it before the bullets caught up to them. They could keep diving beneath the yachts, slowly slipping back to shore, but long before then, the killer would reverse his search, and his light would find them.

"Dive under two more boats," Wolfgang said. "Then surface under the next section of pier. As soon as you do, make some noise. Splash or something. Then dive again."

"What? Why?"

"Trust me," he said, giving her hand a squeeze.

"What about you?"

"I'm gonna get this guy," he said, then turned toward the yacht with the swim ladder.

"Wait!" Megan pulled him back, then ran a hand around his neck and kissed him. "I love you."

He kissed her on the forehead. "I love you, too. Now go."

She dove beneath the surface, kicking toward the shore. Wolfgang turned and slipped out from beneath the pier, treading water to the boat. The yacht floated between himself and the killer, giving him a moment of shelter before the man reached the end of the pier and turned back. Wolfgang pushed off from the pier and grabbed the swim ladder with one hand. He pulled himself up and then placed one foot on the bottom rung, lifting himself slowly so that water draining off his clothes would make minimal noise.

As his head topped the gunwales of the boat, he saw the killer standing at the end of the pier, scanning his light across the smooth surface. Wolfgang slid one leg over the gunwales, then slipped down into the rear of the craft. He crept on his hands and knees to the door that led into the cabin and tried the handle. It was locked.

Think. You're running out of time.

He turned back, crouching to stay below the gunwales, and scanned the rear deck. Other than two benches and a fighting chair, there wasn't much to see.

Wolfgang felt beneath the cushion of the nearest couch and found a storage compartment. Inside the compartment was a tangled mess of beach toys and fishing equipment . . . and a fillet knife. It was long and flimsy, designed to slice open fish, not people, but it would do.

He retrieved the knife, and then he heard Megan's first splash. It came from two boats closer to shore, and at first it sounded like only a fish flipping in the dark. Megan followed it up with a theatrical gasping for air, and Wolfgang ducked behind the fighting chair as footsteps pounded on the pier.

The killer ran by, his gun held at eye level as he dashed for the noise. He passed Wolfgang's yacht without so much as a glance, and Wolfgang slid out from behind the fighting chair. His bare feet hit the pier without a sound, and he broke into a run. The killer was twenty feet ahead, sweeping the light toward the water as he held the gun at the ready. Wolfgang closed half that distance before the killer heard him and stiffened.

The man twisted, desperately directing the gun toward Wolfgang, but it was already too late for him. Wolfgang deflected the gun with a quick sweep of his hand, then they both crashed to the pier.

[4]

The gun spun across the pier, and Wolfgang landed on top of the killer. He flipped the fillet knife point-down and began a sweep toward the man's exposed throat, but the killer jerked his head to one side, and the knife stuck into the pier. The man wrenched his right arm free and drove a gut punch upward. Air whistled between Wolfgang's teeth, and he doubled forward, then fell to the side. He hit the pier on his shoulder and kicked with both legs. His right foot made contact with his opponent's exposed side, but the kick lacked power. The man slid to the side, rolled, and then produced a knife from his belt and rose to his knees. The blade sliced through the air toward Wolfgang's face, and he held up an arm in a primitive attempt at deflection. Steel met flesh with a wicked slicing sound, and Wolfgang screamed. He jerked his arm back as the killer landed on top of him and raised the knife again.

Then the gunshots started: one, two, then three pops from the suppressed handgun. The killer jerked, and the knife fell from his hand, landing on the pier next to Wolfgang. The man fell backward with two holes in his chest and a third in his head.

Megan stood next to Wolfgang, the captured firearm held in both hands. She took a step around his feet, following the killer's body with the muzzle of the gun, and then kicked him in the ribs. He didn't move.

Megan turned to Wolfgang and dropped to her knees. "Wolfgang! Oh my God. Where are you bleeding?"

Wolfgang sat up, clutching his right forearm. It dripped with blood.

"You'll need stitches," she said. "We've got to stop the bleeding."

Megan turned to the body and tore the man's jacket off. Buttons danced across the pier, and she wrapped the garment around Wolfgang's arm, knotting it off. "Hold your arm against your side."

Wolfgang tucked the makeshift bandage against the bullet graze across his ribcage and focused on calming his breathing. A rapidly beating heart would only bleed him out more quickly.

They sat in stunned silence, staring at the killer.

He looked skyward with wide, dead eyes as blood streamed down his face.

Megan held a hand over her mouth and let out a little sob. "Wolfgang . . . Oh my God."

Wolfgang sat up and placed a hand on her back. She crumpled into his shoulder, and the world around him felt fuzzy and distant, as if everything that was so real and sharp only minutes before was now a distant memory. All he could think about were the sounds of those gunshots and the way the knife sliced through his arm.

This man was here to kill us. Not somebody. Us.

"Megan. We've got to go."

She looked up and didn't move, and he shook her arm.

"Megan. Right now!"

She nodded and helped him up, then they ran down the pier and back to the beach. They found a cab not far from the marina, and Megan asked for the nearest ER, but Wolfgang shook his head.

"No. We can't go to the hospital. Take us back to our hotel."

He gave the driver the address and clutched his arm against his side.

"Wolfgang, you need stitches," Megan objected.

He shook his head but wouldn't comment further until they reached the hotel. They stormed through the lobby to the elevator as Wolfgang dripped blood the entire way.

As soon as they reached the room, Wolfgang hurried to the nightstand and picked up his phone with his good hand. "Call Kevin," he said.

"What?"

"Call him! Now."

Wolfgang speed-dialed Edric. He cradled the phone next to his ear and listened as it rang once, five times, then voicemail. Wolfgang hung up and dialed again, waiting through the rings another time. Again, it went to voicemail. He left a message urging Edric to call him back, then shot off a text message just to cover his bases.

"I can't get Kevin," Megan said. She stood next to the window, still wearing nothing but the bikini with blood smudged across her skin.

"Call again!" Wolfgang said as he dialed Lyle.

The phone rang three times, and Wolfgang braced himself for voicemail. Then the phone clicked, and Lyle's sleepy voice spoke over the line.

"Hello? Wolf?"

"Lyle! Where are you?"

"I . . . uh . . . at my house. What—"

"Get up, right now! Do you have a gun?"

"A gun? Wolf—"

"Somebody's coming, Lyle! Get your gun."

Wolfgang heard a soft crashing sound in the background, followed by the tinkle of glass raining over a tile floor. He put the phone on speaker, and Megan hurried next to him.

"Lyle," he hissed. "Do you have a gun?"

"Shut up!" Lyle said.

Wolfgang bit his lip, and nothing but Lyle's heavy breathing filled the phone. He wanted desperately to be there. To say something that would help. To do anything to protect Lyle from whatever was coming.

All he could do was stand uselessly and listen.

"Somebody's coming," Lyle whispered. His breaths grew softer and more measured.

Megan pressed a hand into Wolfgang's and squeezed, and they both held their breath.

There was a clicking sound—maybe a doorknob or a gun being cocked—and then a sharp pop filled the speaker. Wolfgang thought it was a gunshot at first, but the bloodcurdling scream that followed wasn't from a gunshot wound. A loud buzzing filled the phone, electric and sharp, and the screaming continued. Then something heavy hit the floor, and the phone went silent.

"Lyle?" Wolfgang asked.

No answer.

"Lyle!" they said in unison.

The phone beeped, and "Call Failed" appeared on the screen.

Wolfgang and Megan exchanged a look, and suddenly the room felt cold and still.

"I couldn't get Kevin," she whispered. "Edric?"

Wolfgang shook his head. Megan covered her

mouth with one hand, and neither of them spoke. Wolfgang redialed Lyle, but the call went straight to voicemail.

"Somebody's exterminating us," Megan said.

Wolfgang walked to the window and looked out over the distant beach. He scrunched his eyes shut, trying to remember the killer's face. It wasn't a face he knew. It wasn't a face he was supposed to know.

He was an assassin. He was sent here for us.

"Wolfgang, we should call the director."

Wolfgang placed his good arm against the window. The Rolex clicked against the glass, heavy and awkward. He looked at the face and watched the hands ticking methodically. The watch was cracked and smeared with blood.

The director . . .

"Wolfgang!" Megan said. "We have to contact headquarters."

Wolfgang shook his head. "No."

"No?"

"Who knew we were here, Megan?"

"What?"

"Who knew we were in Miami this weekend?"

"I . . . I didn't tell anybody."

"Neither did I. It was a last-minute trip. I was supposed to be in St. Louis."

Megan scrunched her eyebrows together and stared at the carpet. "Right . . ."

"So, how did they find us? How did they know *exactly* where to look? Right down to the marina?"

Wolfgang stepped across the room. His arm throbbed, and he felt woozy, but his head was clear now.

"I don't know. Your phone?"

"I left it on the nightstand. I only took my wallet . . . and this."

Wolfgang unclasped the watch and tossed it onto the bed. Megan picked it up and turned it over, running her thumb across the bloody face.

"I don't understand," she said.

"Turn it over. Open it."

Megan flipped the watch onto its face, exposing the backside of the case, which was smooth and rimless. She placed her thumb against it and twisted. At first it wouldn't budge, but after increased pressure, the cap spun and then fell out.

Wolfgang couldn't see the interior of the watch, but he could tell by the look on her face that he was right.

"A tracking chip?" he asked.

"Where did you buy this?"

"Don't you remember? It was given to me . . . by the director."

Their gazes met, and he saw the disbelief in her eyes, but it was willful disbelief.

Wolfgang took the watch and turned it over. The

GPS chip, powered by a tiny battery, fell out, and then he placed it on the nightstand and used the watch to grind it into pieces. "This isn't a random attack," he said. "Charlie Team is being burned."

5

"That can't be true," Megan said.

Wolfgang stumbled into a chair, still clutching the makeshift bandage to his side. He lifted it to look at the wound on his ribcage and was relieved to see that the bleeding had all but stopped. The bleeding from his arm seemed to have subsided, also.

"You *need* a hospital."

"No. We can't go there. They'll be watching the hospitals."

"You're bleeding! You need stitches."

Wolfgang held up a hand. "Go downstairs and ask for a sewing kit—like you'd use to put buttons on a shirt. Get two or three of them."

"You can't be serious."

"It's our best option. Trust me, okay?"

Megan left the room, and after chugging a bottle

of water, Wolfgang gently unwrapped the bandage. By the time she returned, he'd inspected the severity of the arm cut. It wasn't as bad as he'd initially thought, but it was still severe. It ran along the outside of his arm from two inches below his wrist to two inches above his elbow, about half an inch deep at its worst. He'd need stitches in his arm, but the bullet graze on his ribs could heal without them. Stitches under his arm wouldn't hold anyway.

Wolfgang lay back on the bed and crossed his arm over his chest, exposing the cut. Megan massaged it with a cube of ice, numbing it a little.

"Do you want something from the minibar?" she asked.

Wolfgang shook his head. "Keep the stitches tight and close, okay?"

Megan swallowed, staring at the cut. A trickle of sweat ran off her temple, and the needle trembled as she attempted to thread it.

Wolfgang put his hand on her arm. "Meg?"

She looked up.

"We're alive," he said. "We're gonna be okay."

She nodded a couple times, then licked the end of the thread and deftly stuck it through the needle. A moment later, she began stitching. Wolfgang gritted his teeth with each poke of the needle, but the pain wasn't any greater than he'd already experienced. It took her twenty minutes to run the stitches up the length of his arm, and when he twisted to inspect them, he was impressed. Each stitch was tight and uniform.

"Thank you."

Megan stared at the arm as if she couldn't believe what she was seeing. "You'll need antibiotics," she said. "Some better bandages. And more water."

She hurried to the minibar and returned with two bottles of water. He chugged one as a wave of dizziness passed over him. He wasn't sure how much blood he'd lost, but apparently, it wasn't enough to kill him. At least not yet.

Wolfgang stared at the wall and tried to complete a clear thought. It was impossible to wrap his mind around what had just happened, and it was impossible to comprehend that somebody had tried to kill them. What about Edric? Kevin?

"We have to go," he said. "Right now. Pack."

Wolfgang's phone buzzed from the nightstand. He and Megan froze, watching as the screen lit up with "Unknown Number" flashing across the middle. They exchanged a look, and the phone buzzed again. Wolfgang hit the answer button and immediately switched the phone to speaker mode. They both held their breath.

"Wolfgang?"

"Lyle!" Wolfgang shouted.

"Where are you? No, don't answer that. Your phone may be bugged. Are you safe?"

"Yes," Wolfgang said. "Are you? We heard a scream—"

"The sweet sound of my would-be assassin being electrocuted. My security system got out of hand, though, and did something to my phone. I'm calling you from a backup."

Wolfgang was too strung out to comment on an in-home security system featuring lethal electrocution. "Lyle, listen to me. You've got to get someplace safe, right now. And sweep your clothes. Sweep your car, your gadgets, everything."

"For what?"

"Trackers, Lyle. I found one in my Rolex."

"Rolex? Wait . . . you mean—"

"The one the director gave me. Yes."

"Oh my God . . ." Real fear crept into Lyle's voice.

Wolfgang leaned closer to the phone. "Stay calm. We're going to figure this out."

"What about the others?" Lyle asked. "What about Edric and Kevin?"

Wolfgang exchanged a glance with Megan.

"We haven't been able to reach them. Right now I just want you to get someplace safe, okay?"

"Okay." Lyle's voice wavered, and for the first time, Wolfgang wondered how helpless Lyle must feel. He wasn't strong or fast or good with weapons. Without his computers, Lyle was just another civilian at the mercy of anybody stronger.

"Are we gonna meet?" Lyle asked. "Where should I go?"

Wolfgang's phone vibrated, and a red notification bubble appeared next to his email. He tapped inside and waited for the message to download. It took only a few seconds, and when it finished, the breath caught in his throat.

It was from Edric.

"Wolf?" Lyle said.

"Hold on."

Wolfgang opened the email as Megan crowded in. The message contained only four characters—two numbers with a hyphen in between.

35-7.

"He's alive!" Wolfgang blurted.

"What is it?" Lyle asked.

"Edric's alive! I just got an email."

"Wolfgang, calm down!" Megan said. "Let me see."

Wolfgang passed her the phone, and she frowned. "I don't understand."

"What is it?" Lyle insisted.

Wolfgang ran a hand through his hair. "I can't tell you over the phone. We need to meet."

Wolfgang paced. He needed a way to clue Lyle in without saying it over the phone. Something Lyle would know, but nobody else would. Like Edric's email.

"Lyle, do you remember that time in Moscow

when we were looking at some drawings together? Drawings of a home."

"A home?" Lyle's tone was confused.

"Work with me, Lyle. We were sitting in the hotel room looking at drawings of a house. A *big* house. A house with a lot of chairs."

Silence for a moment.

"Wait," Lyle said. "You mean the house with the big yard?"

"That's the one. I want you to meet me there tomorrow morning at eight a.m. Can you be there?"

"Yeah, I can make it."

"Good. We'll see you then, okay? Watch your back."

Wolfgang hung up and grabbed his bag, throwing his tangled clothes inside.

"That email could be from anybody," Megan said.

"It's not. It's from Edric."

"You can't be sure of that. And thirty-five to seven? What does that even mean?"

"It means Brett Favre had a really bad day, Meg. Get your things. We've got to go."

"Brett Favre? The football player? I don't understand. Where are we going?"

Wolfgang shouldered the bag. "Chicago. We're going to Chicago."

———

Megan and Wolfgang caught the first flight out of Miami to Chicago, arriving in the Windy City at three a.m. and spending a few hours in an airport hotel before taking a cab downtown.

For early April Chicago was brutally cold, altogether unlike Miami. Wind shrieked through the city and ripped between the buildings like an avenging angel, and Wolfgang huddled into his jacket and cast a nervous glance over his shoulder as he walked, checking the faces of the bustling Chicagoans behind him. He wondered if any one of them was a killer. If any one of them was trailing them, ready to open fire at any moment.

"Let's hurry," he said.

Megan was bundled into a jacket and thick pants. Her face was pale under the blast of wind, but the nervousness in her eyes wasn't fear for her own safety. They still hadn't heard from Kevin, and with every passing hour, Wolfgang became less confident they ever would.

Soldier Field sat on the banks of Lake Michigan under the shadow of the city. It was a large and storied stadium, but now that the NFL season had come to a close, the grounds lay quiet and empty. The stadium loomed out of the fog, and in the stiff cold, it wasn't difficult for Wolfgang to take himself back to all those years ago when Edric took him to his first football game—the Packers versus the Bears.

Wolfgang would never forget that day. He was a

kid bouncing between foster homes, but "Uncle" Edric often took him on weekend trips, including this game. Everybody expected the Bears to lose, and because Wolfgang identified with underdogs, he rooted for them. Edric explained the game with each play, and Wolfgang became more engaged as the Bears inexplicably dominated. They shut down Brett Favre's offense and won 35 to 7, the upset of the season.

Chicago went crazy. Popcorn flew in the air, sixty thousand people chanted, and Wolfgang felt the energy of the place in his bones. Edric bought him a Bears jersey on the way out, and just like that, Wolfgang became a life-long fan, attending half a dozen games a year and following the team religiously.

Only it wasn't something he really talked about. That day was special—just for him. Nobody except Edric would know about that game or how significant the final score was.

"Are you sure about this?" Megan asked, placing a hand on his arm.

Wolfgang looked back. He'd explained 35-7 to her on the plane, but she wasn't sold, and he couldn't blame her. It sounded crazy.

"Nobody else knew, Meg," he said. "I never told anybody."

She nodded, and he saw steel creep into her posture. It was the fighting spirit of the woman he loved, and it gave him courage. He gave her hand a squeeze, then they set off toward the stadium.

The greenways and sidewalks that surrounded Soldier Field lay empty, with occasional pieces of trash dancing over the concrete under gusts of wind. They circled to the south side of the stadium, where the concrete entrance rose out of the ground, complete with pillars and an engraved homage to the men and women of the United States armed services. Wolfgang looked up at the flags, then let out a soft, birdlike whistle.

Lyle appeared from behind a tree, hurrying toward them with a backpack slung over one shoulder. When he reached them, he dropped the backpack and threw both arms around Wolfgang in an aggressive hug. Wolfgang stumbled back, surprised by the gesture, then awkwardly wrapped an arm around Lyle's shoulders.

"I'm so glad you're okay," Lyle said.

"I'm so glad you understood my code."

Back in Moscow, Charlie Team had thwarted a terrorist attack that was planned to take place at Soldier Field. He and Lyle had studied schematics of the stadium, notating the location of the weapon.

"It's not really a house," Lyle said. "But it certainly has a lot of chairs."

He released Wolfgang and stepped back with a little shrug.

"Don't I get any?" Megan asked.

Lyle blushed and embraced her, then he knelt beside the backpack and unzipped it. "I drove, so I was able to bring some things."

He withdrew a Smith & Wesson revolver and handed it to Wolfgang, then pulled out a pocket Taser and sheepishly offered it to Megan.

"A Taser?" she said. "Really?"

Lyle shrugged. "I only have the one gun."

"And you gave it to Wolfgang. How very sexist."

Lyle blushed again, and Megan poked him in the ribs.

"Relax, dude. I'm only joking. Give me the Taser."

Lyle shouldered the backpack, then looked toward the stadium.

"I haven't been inside, but one gate is unlocked."

Wolfgang checked the load of the revolver. It was one of Smith's J-frame models, chambered in .38 Special, with five rounds in the cylinder. Wolfgang had never really used revolvers, but he'd heard plenty of stories about how ineffective .38 Special could be.

Edric is here. I won't even need a gun.

Wolfgang pocketed the revolver and squared his shoulders. "I'll go in first. Check it out. Then—"

"No way," Megan said. "We go in together."

Wolfgang acquiesced, then stuck his hand in his pocket and wrapped his fingers around the gun . . . just in case.

———

Lyle led them to the gate he'd found. It was actually a metal door that rolled up, and the bottom was indeed unlocked. Lyle lifted it, and Wolfgang slid in first, followed by Megan.

On the other side was a giant block room, with columns more closely resembling a state capitol than a football stadium. Ticket booths lined one wall, and stairs switched back on either side, leading to different sections of the stands. The massive space was empty, and Wolfgang's footsteps echoed on the flagstone floor. He looked into the shadows at the base of the stairs and tightened his grip on the revolver.

"Where would he be?" Lyle asked.

Wolfgang shook his head, then took a cautious step to his left. He remembered going that way all those years ago at the game. Their exact seat numbers had faded from memory, but he thought they sat on the west side of the stadium, near the end zone.

He led Megan and Lyle past the ticket booths, through an unlocked concourse gate, and into another cavernous hallway. It was dark, with the only light streaming in from passageways that led to seating on the lower levels. Everything was as still as a graveyard and just as cold.

Then Wolfgang heard it—a metallic tap, some-place in the shadows ahead. He placed his finger against the trigger guard of the revolver and held up a hand to Megan and Lyle. They stopped, and he took a step deeper into the shadows.

"Edric?"

No answer. Wolfgang slipped the gun out and took another step around the corner. A second tap echoed from far ahead, behind a bank of stairs that led to higher seating. Wolfgang lifted the gun.

"Edric?"

A shadow broke away from a staircase, twenty yards ahead. It was too dark to make out a face, but as Wolfgang took another cautious step forward, the man left the shadows and stepped into a beam of light pouring through another passageway. Wolfgang froze, ice streaming into his veins. It wasn't Edric.

It was the director.

6

"Megan, Lyle, go!" Wolfgang shouted. He cocked the revolver, sighting along the short barrel at the director's center mass.

The director stood with his hands at his sides and his shoulders relaxed. Wolfgang had only seen him once before in St. Louis, after the Rio operation, but it wasn't a face he'd easily forget. Wolfgang put his finger on the trigger, but the director didn't move.

He just raised one hand, palm out, and spoke softly. "Don't shoot, Wolfgang. I'm alone."

Wolfgang hesitated, then glanced to his left. If there was a sniper in the building, he'd be on the stairwell, where he would have a clean shot of anybody approaching from the unlocked gate. But there wasn't a sniper—at least not that Wolfgang could see.

"Where's Edric?" Wolfgang demanded. "What did you do with him?"

The director lowered his hand and took a step away from the stairs. More light spilled across his body, and Wolfgang could now see that he wore nothing but pants and a loose cotton shirt.

No weapons. No body armor.

"Edric is dead, Wolfgang."

Megan let out a little cry, and something hot burned in Wolfgang's chest. He gritted his teeth and jerked the muzzle of the revolver. "On your knees!"

The director complied without complaint, dropping to his knees and placing both hands behind his head.

Wolfgang closed in, keeping the gun pointed at the director's face, his finger resting on the trigger. "Give me one reason why I shouldn't blow your head off."

"I didn't kill Edric," the director said.

"Nice story. I guess you didn't put the tracker in my watch, either."

The director looked up, confusion crossing his face. "What watch?"

"Save it, you scum."

"Wait. The Rolex?" The director winced. "Shit. That's how he did it."

"Who did it?"

"Nigel. You met him in Rio."

Wolfgang thought back to the airport and the tall

man dressed in all black who presented each member of Charlie Team with a Rolex—a token of the director's gratitude for saving his daughter.

"The guy in black?" Wolfgang asked.

The director nodded once.

"Where's Kevin?" Wolfgang snarled. Footsteps clicked on the flagstones behind him as Megan and Lyle closed in.

"I can't reach him," he said.

"Is he dead?" Megan asked. Her voice wavered, and she clutched the Taser as if she were ready to choke him with it.

The director faced her, his hands still clasped behind his head.

"I don't know, Megan. But . . . probably."

Tears spilled down Megan's cheeks, but it was Lyle who broke first. He slung himself forward, driving a vicious uppercut into the director's jaw. It landed with a sickening crack, and the director fell backward on the concrete with a grunt. Lyle landed on top of him, producing a knife out of nowhere and pressing it against his throat.

"You're lying!" Lyle screamed. "Where are they?"

He pressed with the knife until blood streamed from the director's throat. Wolfgang put a hand on Lyle's shoulder and knelt down.

"Move the knife," he said, placing the muzzle of the gun against the director's temple.

Lyle relaxed on the knife enough so the director could breathe.

"Talk," Wolfgang growled.

"I didn't kill Edric. I didn't kill anyone."

"Who sent the email?" Wolfgang said.

"I did. I knew you'd only come if you believed Edric was alive."

"How did you know about thirty-five to seven?" Wolfgang demanded.

"Edric told me. I was with him when he died. He said you'd know what it meant."

Wolfgang's hand shook. He pressed with the revolver until the director twisted his head under the pressure. Wolfgang didn't want to believe him, but if the email was a ruse designed to lure the surviving members of Charlie Team to their deaths, why was the director here alone? Why hadn't they been gunned down already?

"Why are you here?" Wolfgang said.

"SPIRE has been compromised."

"No shit!" Megan snarled.

"It wasn't me. It was Nigel. Can I sit up, please?"

Wolfgang exchanged a glance with Megan. She shook her head, but something inside Wolfgang told him he was missing most of the puzzle. He could still pull the trigger if the director was lying.

"Back up, Lyle," Wolfgang said.

Lyle shifted backward, and Wolfgang hauled the director up by the shoulder. He dragged him against the nearest wall and motioned for Megan to check his pockets. She found nothing except a wallet and a pair of car keys.

"You've got one minute," Wolfgang said.

The director wiped blood from his throat. "Do you remember that time in Paris?"

"Yes."

"You disarmed a bomb at the top of the Eiffel Tower. A plotted terrorist attack. And then again in Moscow, you guys uncovered and prevented a chemical weapons attack against Chicago."

"Thirty seconds."

The director held up a hand. "Both attacks were plotted by a highly organized group of anarchy terrorists with a singular goal—to topple the world into chaos. You thwarted them, twice."

"We *know* that," Megan said.

"Of course you do. The point is, after the Moscow mission, SPIRE was compromised. Nigel was my right-hand man. He helped me run this company for decades. Hundreds of missions. I trusted him like a brother."

"They bought him?" Wolfgang said.

"No. They converted him."

"What does that mean?" Lyle said.

"Anarchy is like a religion," the director said. "Like Jihad or Nazism. It's a complex, radical form of doctrines that teach that the only way to bring harmony to society is to *upend* society. Bring it to its knees. Anarchists believe that the problem with everything is the established system, and that the system cannot be fixed from the inside. It must be wiped away completely."

"That's madness," Wolfgang said.

"All extremism is madness. That's never stopped it from spreading. Nigel and I had a falling out several months ago when I refused to give him an ownership stake in SPIRE. He's served the company for years, but he's impulsive and irrational—not the kind of leader we need. He was the one who sold the terrorists the location of my daughter while she was in Rio. As revenge, I guess."

The director dropped his head, but Wolfgang wasn't feeling his heartache. Nothing could bring Edric and Kevin back. Nothing could undo the damage being done.

"Are you telling me the Rolex came from Nigel?" Wolfgang said.

"The Rolex came from me, but Nigel must have installed the tracker. He's sold out the entire company, Wolfgang. Alpha and Bravo teams have both gone offline, along with all our independent contractors. To my knowledge, the three of you are all that is left of SPIRE."

A chill entered Wolfgang's blood. He stepped back and lowered the revolver, then looked to Megan. The fear he felt was reflected in her eyes, and even Lyle let out a little sob.

The director just stared at the floor, and when he spoke, his voice was low and soft. "It's worse than you know. Nigel's treachery started as petty revenge. I don't think he ever expected my daughter to be hurt. But even after Rio, he remained in contact with them, and that's when they converted him. I found emails on his computer that went on for months . . . communications with unnamed individuals overseas. After the Paris and Chicago attacks were foiled, they needed a new plan—something that wouldn't fail. Something that would bring the world down. Nigel had an idea."

Everyone waited in silence, and the director wiped his throat again. "Do you remember that time I sent you to Egypt?"

"You mean that thing with the scroll and the tomb?" Wolfgang asked.

"Right. The Egyptians hired us to recover the scroll and protect the location of the tomb because they were concerned that mummified remains may still contain active remnants of an ancient plague."

"We remember," Megan said.

"They were wrong," the director continued. "The remains were far too old and decayed to contain active contaminants, but they did contain DNA samples with visible strands the virus. Think of them like fossils—preserved pictures of what plague cells looked like and how they were constructed."

"What does that mean?" Wolfgang demanded.

"It means that a particularly intelligent scientist may be able to use those pictures to reconstruct a synthetic version of the plague. A custom-designed virus, in other words, with no known cure."

"That was Nigel's idea?" Lyle said.

"No. That was Pascha Koslov's idea."

"Koslov?" Wolfgang said. "The guy from Moscow?"

"Right. The scientist that the terrorists originally used for their planned chemical weapons attack in Chicago. You successfully extracted him from Moscow, but Nigel knew where he was. The emails I read indicate that Koslov was also converted."

"That's impossible," Wolfgang said. "I saw the man. I talked to him. His girlfriend *died* because of these terrorists."

"Did she?" the director asked. "Or did Katya die because of the Russian government, which failed to provide adequate medical treatment, then cruelly imprisoned her and prematurely ended her life? Another victim of the system."

"That's more madness," Megan said.

"I agree, but Pascha Koslov suffers from a unique imbalance of intelligence. He is at once unbelievably brilliant and incredibly vulnerable. Especially after he lost Katya."

"So, now Koslov is working with these people?" Lyle asked.

"Yes, and according to the emails, he's successfully replicated the plague."

"How long have you known about this?" Megan said.

"I uncovered the emails two days ago. It took me a while to understand what I was looking at, but then I called Edric. He was the only one I trusted to help me stop Nigel."

"And then?" Wolfgang pressed. He already knew where this was headed.

The director dropped his gaze. "Edric was at my house when Nigel's men arrived. There were three of them—contract killers from someplace in Europe. Edric got two of them, but the third . . ." He lowered his head. "He was like a son to me. He helped me build SPIRE every step of the way. He was my best operator."

Again the room fell silent, and Wolfgang thought about Edric—the first moment they met back in West Virginia to their last mission together in Tokyo. Edric was more than his boss—more than the man who befriended him when all others abandoned him. Edric was the father figure Wolfgang never had. A man who taught him about football and credit scores and bought him his first beer. Edric was the one who taught Wolfgang what it meant to be good, and he was there to kick his ass when he fell short.

"Where's Nigel?" Wolfgang said.

"Unfortunately, we don't have time to worry

about him. The terrorists are about to strike again, and this time, the CIA knows nothing about it. When I sent you to Tokyo, the mission was to stop the black-market sale of a synthetic gas called Composite Fifteen, which was being developed to subtly distribute medication and vaccinations by air."

"Right," Wolfgang said. "Your point?"

"You were told to bring back samples or documents detailing the construction of Comp Fifteen for the CIA to study—to prevent it from being used as a weapon."

Megan covered her mouth. "Oh God . . ."

"Those documents never made it to the CIA," the director said. "Based on the emails, Edric and I concluded that they fell into the hands of Nigel's terrorists."

Wolfgang lowered the revolver. "And now they're going to use Comp Fifteen as a delivery system for their synthetic plague."

The director nodded. "You three are all that is left of SPIRE. You're the only ones I have left to turn to. I know how hard I've pushed you and how much you've lost, but Charlie Team has one more job to do."

[7]

The director's Gulfstream G550 waited on a private airstrip outside of Chicago. It was identical to the one Charlie Team had used, except the interior featured fewer chairs and a bigger table. A single pilot waited inside—an old man with white hair and a stooped back that, based on first impressions, Wolfgang wouldn't have trusted with a driver's license.

"This is Winston," the director said, squeezing the pilot's shoulders. "He was my contract pilot during my years in the CIA."

Wolfgang regarded Winston without comment, and the old man shuffled into the cockpit. The director hit the button to shut the motorized door, and they all took their seats. Megan sat next to Wolfgang and put a hand on his. She gave it a squeeze and shot him an "Are you sure about this?" look. Wolfgang squeezed back but said nothing.

After leaving Soldier Field, he had little reason to question the director. The man may have been lying, but if he was a terrorist, he would have killed them, and if he was an innocent third party, he never would've risked his life by meeting them in Chicago when they thought he was responsible for Edric and Kevin's deaths. And beyond that, the prospect of a global attack such as the one the director outlined was too chilling to ignore.

The plane jolted, then rolled across the runway. Wolfgang put his belt on, and nobody said anything until the plane broke through the clouds, high above Chicago.

The director cleared his throat. "Details from Nigel's emails are fragmented, at best. Edric and I were able to deduce that the plague has been successfully synthesized and tested on human subjects."

"They used this thing on *people*?" Megan asked.

"It seems so. According to the emails, the weapon has an incubation period of six days, after which the victim experiences cold sweats, shortness of breath, and dizziness. This is followed within twenty-four hours by nausea, vomiting, and increased difficulty breathing. Within the next two days, organ failure begins. Most subjects didn't last more than ten days after being exposed. None survived more than twelve."

"How contagious is it?" Wolfgang asked.

"Extremely. Some of Koslov's notes from the emails indicate that the weapon is five to six times as infectious as a common cold. With an incubation period of six days, you can imagine how quickly it could spread before anybody knew anything about it."

Wolfgang rubbed his temples with his forefinger and thumb. "So, they have a deadly, highly contagious plague with no known cure harnessed to a tasteless, odorless, colorless gas with no known detection method."

"All they need is a venue," Megan said.

"Right." The director reached into a briefcase and withdrew a laptop. A moment later, a TV screen next to his chair illuminated with a mirror image of the laptop screen, and he clicked through images of men and women in suits. "Nigel's emails contain no information about the location of the attack, but we have a pretty good idea where it's going down. The men and women you're looking at are representatives of China, Russia, Japan, the United Kingdom, the United States, and about six other nations currently assembled at a summit in Sydney, Australia, to discuss a new international trade agreement. The summit was sponsored by the governments of China and Japan, and both of their presidents are actually on-site, along with almost two hundred diplomatic representatives from other countries."

"What's the itinerary?" Wolfgang asked.

"It began last Monday and will conclude tomorrow night with a show at the Sydney Opera House. Edric and I believed that the opera house is the most logical target of the attack."

The director continued to scroll through images of foreign diplomats, but Wolfgang wasn't watching. It didn't matter who was there—it only mattered that if they were infected, they would spread the virus around the world in a matter of days, infecting the hearts of key governments in the process. By the time the first fly dropped, it would be much too late to stop. Hundreds of millions would die in the first weeks.

"What's your plan?" Wolfgang asked.

The director looked away from the laptop and ran a hand over his face. Wolfgang noticed how tired he looked—like he hadn't slept in weeks. Black bags hung under his eyes, and his body looked broken, as if he'd been hit by a truck.

"I don't have a plan," he said. "Actually . . . I was hoping you might have one."

Wolfgang exchanged a look with Megan and Lyle. They both seemed edgy and out of sorts. Only hours before, he'd thought about making love with Megan in their Miami hotel room. He'd thought about walking down the beach and dancing at the restaurant. He'd thought about the ring in his pocket and how he'd been only moments away from dropping to one knee. If he had, she'd probably be dead right now. And he might be, also.

Wolfgang got up and walked to the minibar at the tail of the plane. There were no Sprites in the fridge—something Edric always kept around for him. He settled on a bottle of water and chugged half of it before turning back to the director. "Where are we headed?"

The director shrugged. "West. I think the flight plan is for Los Angeles, but honestly, I just wanted us in the air. It's unlikely that Nigel will divert additional resources to tracking you down. My guess is that he deployed assassins against Charlie Team to cover his tracks, or maybe because the other terrorists demanded revenge."

"You're sure about all of this?" Megan asked. "You're sure about Koslov, and the plague, and Sydney?"

"All I know is what I read in Nigel's emails and that he tried to kill me. For what it's worth, Edric believed it."

"So you say," Lyle said.

The director faced him. "Edric was as dear to me as my own daughter. You don't have to believe me, but it's true."

Wolfgang finished his water. "We believe you. What was Edric's plan?"

The director dug a pair of reading glasses out of his

briefcase, then returned to the laptop. "Edric obtained a set of blueprints for the opera house. Construction began in 1959, but there have been a lot of updates and some substantial remodeling. The main concert hall is where the summit show is set to take place tomorrow night. The hall seats almost twenty-seven hundred people and is expected to be at capacity. The roof is padded and designed to reflect and magnify acoustics, which unfortunately makes it ideal for containing a gas. Sound waves are likely to propel the agent back down to the floor, recirculating it multiple times."

"Do you have a theory on how the gas will be introduced to the hall?" Megan asked.

"HVAC system, probably. If it were me, I'd compress the weapon into some manner of pressurized tank, then pump it into an air duct. It could be deployed electronically or via a timer."

Wolfgang said, "So we have to get inside the opera house and find it, before it's deployed."

"Right, and that's the problem. If we'd known about this a week ago, we might've been able to get inside. As it is, that place is bottled up tighter than the White House. Coordinated security from a dozen countries is on-site, and nobody gets in or out without extensive clearance."

"If they're so on edge, they should be easy to convince of an impending attack," Megan said.

"You'd think, wouldn't you? I've already reached

out to the CIA, DHS, FBI . . . every contact I have. Nobody believes me."

"That's stupendous," Lyle said. "Call them again. Threaten the attack yourself, if you have to. There's got to be a way to make them call off the opera."

"It's not that simple. This summit is huge. It's quite possibly the biggest single diplomatic event since the Millennium Summit in 2000. Extreme amounts of political capital are at stake, and no one country is willing to freak out and raise a security concern. If it turned out to be a false alarm, the narrative would quickly swing against them. They'd be accused of intentionally sabotaging the summit."

"So, instead, they'll risk Armageddon," Lyle said.

"Denial is a strange and powerful thing. Even the world's most brilliant leaders aren't immune to it. The point is that nobody's going to help us. We have to stop it ourselves."

Megan clenched her fist. "Which we can't do if we can't get inside."

"Right. That's the problem Edric and I hit."

Wolfgang rubbed his chin. He paced the length of the plane, stopping now and again to work his jaw to clear his ears. The G550 must've been flying close to max altitude, and the pressure change was getting to him. He tried to put himself in Edric's shoes. For years he'd leaned on Edric—maybe more than he realized. Edric was always there to fall back on—

always there to call on for advice. Wolfgang made plans and acted independently, but in the back of his mind, he knew he had support if he needed it. But not now. Now he was on his own. Megan and Lyle were there, sure, but this problem was his to solve.

Wolfgang rested a hand on the overhead cargo rack and thought about Sydney. He thought about the security and who would be there. He thought about the impossibility of getting inside.

"We need somebody to believe us," Lyle said. "That's our best bet."

"Lyle, I've got almost thirty years of experience in the intelligence sector," the director said. "None of my contacts believe me. Who do you suggest we call?"

"I know somebody," Wolfgang said, turning around.

"Who?" the director asked.

"Somebody who *will* believe us. Somebody who has sufficient clearance to get us inside the opera house."

"*Who*?" everyone said in unison.

Wolfgang indulged in a bitter smile. "An old friend from Mother Russia . . . Ivan Sidorov."

8

They landed in Los Angeles to refuel, and then the G550 turned toward Sydney. Winston put the plane on autopilot, and Wolfgang heard him snoring from the cockpit, but all things considered, the old codger's piloting methods felt the lesser threat at hand.

They shut the windows and turned down the cabin lights, and the director collapsed into an exhausted sleep in the back of the plane. Lyle found a laptop and went to work on a set of blueprints from the opera house, mapping out routes to the HVAC system and possible deployment locations for the weapon. He leaned close to the computer and worked at a feverish pace, taking notes on a scratch pad and not getting up for hours at a time.

Wolfgang and Megan sat by themselves near the cockpit, snuggled together in one of the wider chairs.

They left their window shade open and watched the sun glimmering over the right-hand wing of the plane, slowly setting to the northwest. The G550 cruised southwest at over five hundred miles per hour, slowing the sun's descent to a crawl.

Megan rested her head against his chest and gave his hand a squeeze. "Do you really think he'll help us?"

"Ivan?"

Megan nodded, still watching the sun. Wolfgang thought about Ivan and the phone call he made to Moscow an hour previously. Ivan Sidorov was a top agent in the Russian SVR, and he and Wolfgang had met on two occasions—both of which resulted in significant fireworks. The two of them were the furthest thing from friends, but Ivan had been hunting these anarchists just as long as Wolfgang had been thwarting their attacks. If anybody would believe them, it was Ivan Sidorov, but Wolfgang hadn't been able to get him on the phone. Nobody in Moscow would admit that Ivan even existed, let alone forward the call. Somebody eventually agreed to take a message, but that was it.

"He'll help us if he gets the message," Wolfgang said.

"How can you be sure?"

He sighed. "Did you ever hear that Sting song called 'Russians'?"

"I think so."

"It was about the Cold War. Sting said he hoped the Russians loved their children, because it was our best hope of avoiding a nuclear holocaust."

"You think Ivan has children?"

"No. I mean, maybe. That's not really the point. I just think Ivan's a good egg. I think he cares about his people. I trust in that."

They both fell silent, watching as the sun faded beneath the clouds. Orange turned to red with streaks of purple, as irregular and elegant as a water-color painting. Above the clouds was perhaps the most beautiful sunset Wolfgang had ever seen—peaceful and still, uninterrupted by humanity with all of its noise and conflict.

"Remember that time in Tokyo?" Megan said. Her voice was as soft as a summer wind.

Wolfgang stroked her arm. "How could I forget?"

"Remember when we woke up in the hotel, just you and me?"

"You were morning shy."

She smiled. "I remember lying in bed with you, talking about the future. Do you remember what you said?"

She twisted until her grey eyes looked up at him. They were deeper and more sincere than he'd ever seen, as open and unguarded as a child's. He held her gaze and felt a hush over his soul that reminded him of their first kiss—something so powerful and imme-diate that it shut out the world around them.

"I said that if I could have a quieter life with you, I'd quit SPIRE."

She said nothing, and they just stared at each other. It was more perfect a moment than their first kiss—more powerful than the first time they made love. Just them. Alone.

"Is that offer still on the table?" Megan said.

This is your moment.

Wolfgang slipped his hand into his pocket and felt for the ring. It was still there, nestled amid the lint. Waiting. He drew it out and held it between two fingers, allowing the setting sun to glimmer off the solitaire diamond, then he lifted it so she could see.

"It is if you'll have me."

Megan's eyes watered, and for a moment, she just stared at the ring. The sun bathed her skin in gold, and tears slid down her cheeks. She swallowed, and then she nodded.

Wolfgang slid out of his seat, dropping to one knee and holding the ring up. Megan smiled brighter than the sun, and Wolfgang felt something wet slip down his own cheek. She held out her left hand, and he slid the ring on. It fit perfectly.

Wolfgang got up and kissed her, holding her tight. She laid her head against his chest as the last light faded through the window, and Wolfgang knew his proposal couldn't have been more perfect on any beach in the world.

At last, he let her go, and they both sat down

again. Wolfgang heard a sniffing sound from the back of the plane and stuck his head into the aisle.

Lyle hid behind his laptop, but Wolfgang saw a tissue.

"Lyle?" he said.

Lyle's face appeared over the top of the computer. His glasses were a little foggier than normal, and his cheeks red. "Shut up," he said. "I'm not crying. You're crying."

The G550 touched down outside of Sydney fifteen hours after they left Los Angeles. It was now early morning, but because they had crossed the International Date Line during their flight, it was also the next day on the calendar. The day of the opera.

The concluding summit show would take place at eight p.m., local time. Before then Wolfgang and what was left of Charlie Team had to locate the weapon, disable and remove it, and deal with any terrorists they found along the way—all without sufficient weapons, gear, or guaranteed access into the opera house.

Wolfgang stepped out onto the tarmac and looked up at the sky. Sydney was a lot warmer than Chicago, and the sun felt good on his skin. Even so, he couldn't help but wonder if this would be the last sunrise he would see.

Megan and Lyle followed him down the steps, carrying nothing but a cardboard box with a couple pistols, bottled water, some cash, and the laptop, which Lyle described as an "under-built piece of crap." The director had left his mansion in Kansas City in too great a hurry to collect anything more, and none of Charlie Team's auxiliary resources were available, either, including an exfiltration plan or any kind of vehicle. They were basically on their own, with nothing but their wits.

And, hopefully, one rogue Russian.

The director hurried down the steps and looked apologetically at the box. "I'm sorry. I know it's not much. It's all I have."

"It's fine," Wolfgang said. He put an arm on the director's shoulder and gave it a squeeze. "I appreciate everything. You should go home now."

"What?" The director frowned. "You can't be serious."

"We are," Megan said.

The three of them had discussed the subject while the director slept on the plane, and the decision had been unanimous. Wolfgang believed the director about Edric and Nigel, but that didn't mean the director brought any useable skillsets to the table or wouldn't complicate things with Ivan, assuming he showed up.

"Go home and look after your daughter," Wolfgang said. "If worse comes to worst, you should be with her."

The director hesitated, but Wolfgang saw the slump in his shoulders. He'd done everything he could. Now it was time for Charlie Team to finish the job.

"I'm deeply honored to have known all of you," the director said. "If anybody can fix this, Charlie Team can."

Wolfgang offered his hand, and the director shook it. His grip was firm and gave Wolfgang a little more confidence in his sincerity.

"Godspeed, Wolfgang." He turned and ascended the stairs.

The plane's engines wound back to life, and they watched the G550 arc away into the eastern sky.

Wolfgang put a hand on Lyle's and Megan's shoulder and bowed his head. He'd never prayed before. He wasn't even sure what it meant to pray, exactly, but somehow, he felt they needed a moment.

After a few seconds of silence, Wolfgang drew a deep breath and squeezed their shoulders. "For Edric," he said. "And for Kevin."

Lyle gritted his teeth. "Let's get these bastards."

They turned to the box and unpacked the meager gear. Wolfgang tucked a pistol into his jacket, and they divided up the water and cash.

"We'll go into the city," Wolfgang said. "Book a

hotel and set up a command center. Then we'll worry about getting into the opera."

"How far is the walk?" Lyle said.

"I don't believe we'll be walking," Megan said, shielding her eyes with one hand. "Look."

Wolfgang followed her line of sight and watched as two black SUVs appeared at the end of the landing strip, dust clouds shimmering in their wake as they roared toward the knot of new arrivals. He couldn't make out the plates, but as the vehicles drew closer, he recognized them as Mercedes G-Class SUVs.

Not Americans. Probably not Australians, either.

The SUVs ground to a halt fifty yards out, and men in black suits spilled out, guns drawn. Three of them huddled next to the SUVs, guns resting against the hoods, while three more marched straight toward them. On either side, a man with a pistol walked, and in between them strode a big man with broad shoulders, jet-black hair, and chunky features only a mother would love.

SVR officer Ivan Sidorov.

Wolfgang took a step in front of the team, keeping his arms hanging loose at his sides, away from his pistol. Ivan held up a hand, and the two men next to him stopped, allowing him to step in front of them until he stood only feet away from Wolfgang.

Ivan wore dark sunglasses, and he absently chewed on a toothpick. It flicked back and forth across his wide mouth, and Wolfgang noticed the unnatural cant of his oversized nose—the result of a toilet seat bashing it back in Paris.

Ivan let out a soft, slow laugh. It began as a rumble in the back of his throat but soon exploded into a full-on roar. Wolfgang said nothing, waiting until Ivan took the toothpick out of his mouth and slowly shook his head.

"Hell's angels, Amerikos. You really do have stones."

9

Wolfgang held out his hand and winced when Ivan took it, gripping hard enough to crush brick.

Ivan gestured to the swollen cut running up the outside of Wolfgang's arm, still held closed by Megan's stitches. "You need some vodka for that, Amerikos?"

Wolfgang did his best to return the grip and kept his head up. "I need blood for it."

Ivan grunted, then looked at Lyle and Megan for the first time. He replaced the toothpick in his mouth, then shouted something in Russian to his men. One of them said something back, his tone sultry. Ivan shot him a look that would curdle milk, and the five men holstered their pistols and climbed into one of the SUVs.

Ivan held out his hand to the other vehicle. "Please. Join me."

Wolfgang led the way to the SUV. He held a back door open and let Lyle and Megan climb in across the back seat. Ivan took shotgun and said something in Russian to the driver. The SUV rumbled off, trailed by its companion.

"When headquarters in Moscow gave me your message, they didn't tell me who it's from," Ivan said. "But I know. There is only one Amerikos crazy enough to call in a terrorism tip to Moscow and then fly to site of the attack."

"Did you get my gift?" Wolfgang asked.

"You mean the thumb drive you mailed me with details of the Chicago attack?"

Wolfgang nodded.

"Da. It was good gift, Amerikos. Like my birthday. We find many of the terrorists planning the attack. They are currently enjoying some . . . Russian justice. Unfortunately, however, these anarchists are like a virus. You inoculate one strain, and already another is ready to infect you."

"So you believe us, then?"

Ivan made a little laugh and chewed on the toothpick as he watched the Australian landscape rush by. It was green, with rolling hills and small clusters of suburbia, not altogether unlike California. A quiet place. A place to raise your family and attend sporting events. A place that didn't deserve to be torn apart by an incurable plague.

"Two days ago, Russian intelligence receives tip that the scientist involved in the chemical weapons plot has established laboratory in Canada," Ivan said. "He has changed name, but when he ordered a particular controlled chemical, Canadian authorities recorded his identification, and the picture matches."

"Pascha Koslov," Wolfgang said.

"Da."

"We helped him escape Moscow. We thought he was a victim."

Megan shot Wolfgang an alarmed glance, but he held up a hand. His gut told him it was best to be honest with Ivan. The Russian looked into the rearview mirror. Wolfgang couldn't be sure because of the sunglasses, but he thought Ivan was staring right at him.

"Da," he said. "I know."

The SUV rumbled along for a while longer. Wolfgang wanted to press, but at this stage, they were pretty much at Ivan's mercy. The Russians hadn't taken their weapons, so he didn't think they were being driven to prison. He'd trusted Ivan this far, and he may as well keep trusting.

"There is word in English I can never remember. It means . . . thing that is not but could be. Like imaginary circumstances."

"Hypothetical?" Wolfgang said.

Ivan snapped his fingers. "Da! Hypothetical. I should write that down."

A few miles flashed by, then Ivan took the toothpick out of his mouth and licked his lips. "Hypothetical, Amerikos. Let us say there is a Russian. He works for Moscow, hunting terrorists."

"Hypothetically," Wolfgang said.

"Da, hypothetical only," Ivan said, holding up a finger. "Let us say this man receives tip from crazy Amerikos that attack is happening at . . . a concert, for instance."

"Okay."

"Let us say that our Russian has received other intelligence tips and he is persuaded to believe the crazy Amerikos."

Wolfgang leaned forward a little. "Yes . . ."

"So, our Russian would call his bosses. Tell them about potential attack. Ask for permission to bring Russian justice against the terrorists."

"And what would they say? Hypothetically."

Ivan ground the toothpick between his teeth. "They would say no, Amerikos. Because the summit—I mean, the *concert*—is very important for politics, and they do not want to risk international embarrassment."

The director was right. Everybody's too chicken to call it.

Wolfgang turned to Megan and Lyle, who both sat tense but quiet.

He gritted his teeth. "I guess our hypothetical Russian has no stones, then. I guess he's a coward."

Ivan sat bolt upright, twisting his head around the seat. "In hypothetical only, Amerikos!"

Wolfgang folded his arms.

Ivan flushed a little red, then returned to his seat. He rolled the toothpick between his fingers and sucked his teeth. "One more hypothetical, Amerikos."

"Okay."

"What if the Russian's hands are tied, but he believes there is a threat? What would he do?"

Wolfgang leaned forward. "He'd accidentally help the Amerikos get into the concert. And then he'd stand back."

———

The Russians weren't all that different from Charlie Team in the way they set up headquarters. Ivan had rented adjoining suites in a downtown hotel, and his men were spread about with computers and coffee cups, shouting to one another in Russian and taking phone calls. There were guns everywhere. Wolfgang had never seen so many weapons in one place—rifles, shotguns, pistols. It was like a boiler room for spec ops soldiers.

"I thought you were in the foreign intelligence

service," Wolfgang said, standing near the door with a cup of black coffee in one hand.

Ivan smirked. "As you say in America, I have many heads."

"Hats, Ivan. You wear many hats."

"Yes, this is what I mean."

Ivan snapped his fingers and rattled off some Russian. The room became immediately still as everybody listened. When Ivan finished, the work resumed, and he led Wolfgang, Lyle, and Megan across the bedroom of one suite into a giant bathroom, then closed the door.

The noises outside faded, and Ivan pulled at his tie. "Okay, Amerikos. Here is deal. I tell my people you are local police advising on security for our diplomats. They know better, but they won't ask questions. I can get you inside the opera, but after this, you are Long Ranger, understand?"

"Lone Ranger. Got it."

"Let me be clear. If you are caught, I cannot help you. I have many hats, but one of them is not God. Also, I know you have weapons. You must leave them here."

Wolfgang shook his head. "No good, Ivan. We need the guns."

Ivan muttered something dark in Russian. "You do not understand. This is not about what you need. This is about what is possible. Security at opera house is very tight, and there are metal detectors and dogs. I can get you inside, but not with weapons."

Wolfgang saw uncertainty in Megan's eyes, but she just nodded. Without Ivan's help, they'd never get inside at all, and then it didn't matter how many guns they had.

"Okay. No guns," Wolfgang said. "How will we get inside?"

"I will give you Russian security pass. It will get you through checkpoints, but some of the rooms in the opera are still locked, and there are cameras. I have no solution for this."

"I've got that covered," Lyle said.

Ivan regarded him a minute, then grunted. "If you say so." He turned back to Wolfgang. "One last thing, Amerikos. Australian security has the opera on total lockdown until seven p.m. This is the earliest I can get you in."

"Seven? Ivan, that's an *hour* before the show."

Ivan grunted. "So you must work quickly."

"Work quickly?" Wolfgang took a step closer. "Ivan, the weapon could already be deployed by then. People could be infected. Are you hearing me?"

Ivan cursed and threw both hands up. "I do all I can, Amerikos. I am not miracle worker. Unless you can convince the Australians otherwise, you will not get in before seven."

Wolfgang could see apprehension in his team—a

respect for the imminence of death only acquired by having faced these terrorists before.

Megan put a hand on his arm. "It's okay, Wolf. We've got this."

Wolfgang turned back to Ivan and held both hands palm out. "You're right, Ivan. Thank you. I know you did everything you could."

Ivan shrugged the gratitude away. "It is nothing, Amerikos."

He produced a fresh toothpick from his pocket and slipped it between his lips, chewing for a moment. Wolfgang had the impression there was something else on his mind.

"There is other thing," Ivan said.

"What?"

"It is small matter. But I would be remiss not to say that if you find this weapon, Russia will be happy to safely remove and destroy it. Just call me."

Wolfgang laughed. "Seriously?"

Ivan smirked. "Is duty of good Russian to be of service to his country."

"If we find this weapon, Ivan, you'd better hope you have *time* to remove it. But you're not taking it back to Russia. Just because we understand each other doesn't mean I trust your country."

Ivan made a noncommittal grunt, then led them out of the suite and down the hallway to another smaller room with only a bed and a table. Two black suits lay on the bed—a man's and a woman's—both matching those worn by Ivan's men down the hall. Black shoes sat at the foot of the bed, and a paper bag full of fragrant food sat on the table.

"I thought you would be hungry," Ivan said.

Wolfgang nodded his thanks, realizing he hadn't eaten since the night before in Miami.

"I will send photographer to take your pictures for ID cards," Ivan said. "And a car to take you across town. Anything else?"

"That's plenty," Wolfgang said, offering his hand. "Thank you."

Ivan deployed that bone-crushing grip again. "Good luck, Amerikos. For all that is good in the world, I hope you are wrong." Then Ivan left the room.

For a moment, the three of them stood awkwardly next to the bed, and Wolfgang knew Megan and Lyle were probably thinking about the same thing he was—Edric, and Kevin, and all the times Charlie Team had assembled in a hotel room to plan out a mission or salvage a wrecked one. It wasn't difficult for him to picture Kevin knocking back whiskey at the minibar and Edric pacing around, ranting about things with his tie hanging loosely from his neck.

But this time, it was just them. The room felt still and empty, and Wolfgang had the sudden impression that Lyle and Megan expected him to fill the void. To step into Edric's shoes. It was an impossible role to fill, like assuming the presidency after Lincoln was shot, or taking the stage after Elvis died.

What would Edric do right now? What would he say?

Wolfgang had an idea, and he walked to the nightstand next to the bed. He found a pen in the drawer, took it to one of the large white walls next to the TV, then uncapped it with his teeth. Without comment, he wrote words on the wall: Sydney, opera house, terrorist plot, end of the world. He connected them all with a maze of random lines, then stepped back to admire his handiwork. When he looked back at Megan and Lyle, both of them were tearing up, but they were also smiling.

Wolfgang capped the pen and shrugged a little. "Felt like we needed a little of Edric's marker board."

Megan nodded and wiped her face with one sleeve. Wolfgang pulled them both into the circle again and put his hands on their shoulders. "Who gets it done?"

"Charlie gets it done," they said in unison.

"Damn right. Let's kick some ass."

10

"Charlie Eye, all systems check," Lyle said.

Wolfgang adjusted his tie as he stepped out of the cab. The Russian earpiece didn't quite fit his ear, and he kept wanting to adjust it but knew it would draw attention. His jacket was a little too large and the shoes a bit narrow. But all things considered, Ivan had done a hell of a job outfitting Charlie Team on short notice.

"This is Charlie One," Megan said. "I've got you, loud and clear." She climbed out of the other side of the car, brushing her hair behind her ear and fidgeting with her pantsuit. She didn't like the cut, and the arms were too long, but Wolfgang still thought she looked gorgeous. With her natural mild complexion and deep red hair, he thought she even looked a little Russian.

One badass fiancée.

"Charlie Lead?" Lyle said. "Are you there?"

Wolfgang's mind ratcheted back to the present, and he felt a sudden wave of surreal discomfort.

I'm Charlie Lead.

He cleared his throat. "Charlie Lead . . . loud and clear."

Wolfgang tightened his tie, then joined Megan on the other side of the cab and set off down the sidewalk. All around them, downtown Sydney reached for the sky in glistening glory, each glass-faced building lit like a Christmas tree as night fell. A brisk wind blew off the Pacific, but it wasn't like the relentless wrath of a Chicago wind. Sydney was warm and vibrant, with crowds of people from around the world filling the streets and chattering excitedly between restaurants and bars.

Charlie Team spent the entire afternoon studying blueprints of the opera house and mapping out the most likely location of the weapon. With remodels and unpredictable shifts in security, it was impossible to make more than an educated guess about where to look, but they all agreed that the most logical place to position the weapon would be somewhere in the opera house's HVAC system. On a warm night with a full house, the opera would run the air conditioning, pumping cool air into the main concert hall via discreet vents in the floor.

Accessing the HVAC system wouldn't be easy, as it was all housed in a secure basement beneath the main building, along with electrical and plumbing controls for the entire facility. But Lyle had successfully hacked into the opera's base-level security system, which would allow him to monitor hallways and rooms via security cameras, as well as electronically unlock certain doors. With luck, that would be enough to give them access to the basement.

After that, Wolfgang and Megan were on their own. Lyle could do nothing about the droves of international security forces on-site or the threat of the actual terrorists making a play to stop them. Unarmed and alone, Wolfgang and Megan would simply have to figure it out.

"T-minus seventy-five minutes to the opera," Lyle said. "The Chinese president is en route."

"Copy that," Wolfgang said. He took the lead on the sidewalk, breaking through the crowd with the ice-cold indifference of how he imagined a Russian would walk. According to their fake ID cards, Megan and Wolfgang were members of some state-level security agency that Wolfgang had never heard of. Ivan admonished them to speak as little as possible and lean on the legitimacy of the identification. It seemed like a shoestring plan at best.

"Don't walk so fast," Megan said. "I have short legs."

Wolfgang slowed, and as Megan caught up, she shot him a sultry look. "Trying to dump me already?"

He grinned. "Is it too late?"

"Talk to the ring, buddy."

They left downtown and moved into the harbor district, taking Macquarie Street past the Government House and a row of high-rise condominiums. In the distance, Wolfgang heard the gentle wash of the Pacific Ocean lapping against a rocky seashore, and the air tasted of salt. A roundabout lay directly ahead, and security lined the street on all sides, while motorcycle cops buzzed back and forth along the street, waving at pedestrians to stand back. All the dignitaries attending the summit finale would arrive via Macquarie Street, the only direct access to the opera house.

Wolfgang led Megan through the growing crowd to the end of the street, then followed the sidewalk around the roundabout before ascending a short flight of brick steps. The opera house appeared all at once, rising skyward in majestic glory with the ocean as its backdrop. Wolfgang had seen plenty of pictures, but in person, the building was much larger and more elegant than he'd imagined. Each of its sail-shaped roofs reached skyward before dipping down to point out to sea, illuminated by purple lights that gleamed off polished stone and shimmered on quiet harbor waters.

The building was more a work of art than a structure, more a hallmark of Australian culture and pride than a concert hall. It was beautiful in every sense of the word, and Wolfgang thought that if it were another night, with the fate of the world not on the line, this might be a pretty good spot for a Tokyo-style kiss.

"Charlie Eye, we're on-site," Wolfgang said.

"Copy that, Charlie Lead. Chinese motorcade is five minutes out."

Red and blue lights flashed in the distance as a gathering roar of cheering onlookers welcomed the motorcade. Wolfgang motioned for Megan to hurry, and they broke across the brick-paved surface of the forecourt leading up to the opera house. Every few yards, they ascended another flight of steps, and the building grew larger, blocking out the horizon.

It was actually three buildings—a restaurant with two miniature sails built on top sitting to the left, a mid-sized structure with four larger sails sitting to the right and housing some kind of theater, and the primary building with its four massive sails front and center. It was the middle building that contained the main concert hall and would host that night's event. The strongest security would be focused around the concert hall, along with the north foyer and bar built into the backside of the building. Here the guests would gather and mill about over the next hour, prior to entering the concert hall.

A security post guarded the side entrance to the middle building, policed by ten men in black suits and two German Shepherds with personalities as dynamic as cinder blocks. A couple opera house workers and national security personnel were busy checking themselves in, and Megan and Wolfgang slipped into separate lines to pass through quickly.

A chubby Australian cop waited for Wolfgang next to a metal detector, offering a warm smile as he approached. "G'day, mate. Can I see some credentials, please?"

Wolfgang handed him his Russian ID card and waited as the cop scanned it into a computer.

"Warm night, isn't it?" the cop said. "I always say a warm night is best for the opera. Really brings out the tone of the organ, you know?"

Wolfgang smiled and tried not to fidget.

The cop tapped something into the computer, then squinted at the ID. "You're Russian security, mate?"

Wolfgang nodded.

"Don't say much, do you?"

Not when I don't speak a word of Russian, mate.

He tapped on the computer again. "Okay, well, you're all clear. Just have to sweep you down."

Wolfgang stepped through the metal detector, thinking about his pistol back in the hotel room. Ivan was right—there was no chance of sneaking it through security, but he still felt naked without it.

The cop patted him down with a thoroughness that bordered on molestation, and Wolfgang glanced sideways to see Megan undergoing the same procedure. Suddenly, one of the dogs woofed. It was a deep, irritated sound, and when he traced it to its originator, he saw a shepherd staring at him, his ears stiff. The dog lifted a lip and took a half-step toward him.

Oh, great.

The cop finished his search, and Wolfgang stepped quickly away from the metal detector. He hadn't made it five feet before the cop called after him.

"Hold up there!"

Wolfgang almost ran, but Megan was still being patted down. If he ran now, it would blow the whole thing. He looked back, avoiding eye contact with the dog.

"You forgot your ID, mate," the cop said, holding out the card.

Wolfgang smacked himself in the forehead and took it with a grateful nod. Megan cleared security, and they started back toward the opera house, ascending the last row of steps and approaching a row of glass doors. A bellman dressed in a white tuxedo offered them a little bow and held the door. They stepped into a rush of cold air conditioning, and Wolfgang adjusted his tie, suddenly wondering if the weapon was already in place, pumping lethal doses of an untreatable plague into the air.

No. Nigel and his crew of terrorists would wait to deploy the weapon until everybody was inside the concert hall. It made more sense.

"You good?" Wolfgang said. Megan nodded, and Wolfgang adjusted the uncomfortable Russian earpiece. "Charlie Eye, we just entered the building."

"Copy that, Charlie Lead. You should see a bank of elevators directly ahead, with hallways leading to your right and left. Take the right-hand hallway, and follow it around the east side of the building. I should have you on camera, then."

"Copy that."

Wolfgang turned to the right, he and Megan dodging between servers, bellmen, and security personnel as they took another flight of stairs, then wound their way onto a wide, red-carpeted hall. Signs pointed the way into the concert hall or up stairwells to the various elevated wings, where the most distinguished dignitaries would sit. Chinese security dressed in black suits ran back and forth and spoke into wrist-mounted mics. In the background, the bustle and roar of the president's arriving motorcade had reached a crescendo, and nobody paid any attention to the two pseudo-Russians marching down the hall like they owned the place.

Lyle said, "Smile for the camera, Charlie Lead."

Wolfgang impulsively glanced up but didn't see the security camera.

"Fifty yards ahead, the hallway terminates at a stairwell, and another hallway branches to the right.

Follow the second hallway about twenty yards until you hit a bank of metal doors."

Wolfgang quickened his stride, aware that Megan was straining to keep up. A silent clock in his head ticked methodically, reminding him that with each passing second, their likelihood of failure increased. They made the turn, then reached the metal doors. Wolfgang heard the electronic lock disengage right before he pushed, and then he and Megan crossed off the red carpet and onto a linoleum floor hallway with utilitarian doors on either side.

"Fourth door on your right," Lyle said. "I've got the lock."

Wolfgang approached the door and put his hand on the latch, but it wouldn't budge. "Charlie Eye?"

"Working . . ."

Wolfgang cast Megan a look. He heard footsteps from around a bend in the hallway, growing louder by the second to match the tempo of Lyle's typing.

"Charlie Eye?" Wolfgang said again. The door handle still wouldn't turn.

"I'm ordering the unlock," Lyle said. "Something's jammed."

Wolfgang tried the handle again. The footsteps around the corner were almost there, and he wondered if they were opera house workers or Chinese security. What excuse did he have for being there?

"Still jammed," Lyle said.

Wolfgang clenched his fist and smashed it against the door handle. Pain shot up his arm, throbbing around the swollen cut from the hit man's knife. Then the door lock clicked, and Wolfgang shoved it open. They slipped into the shadows just as the footsteps turned the corner in the hallway. Wolfgang held his breath as two Chinese men in black suits hurried past.

"You good?" Lyle asked.

"Copy that," Wolfgang said.

Megan put a hand on his arm and gave him a reassuring squeeze.

"Okay, I don't have you on camera anymore, but there should be a stairwell at your back, leading downward."

The stairs were wide, built of concrete, and switched back on themselves every ten steps as they led beneath the concert hall and dressing rooms, and to the basement of the opera house. After two flights, Wolfgang checked in with Lyle but received a garbled response.

"We're losing him," Wolfgang said. "Lyle, if you can hear us, you're breaking up."

". . . continue . . . door . . ."

Wolfgang tore the earpiece out and hurried forward with Megan on his heels. They traversed two more levels, then reached another set of metal doors with a keycard scanner next to them. A security camera pointed out of the corner next to the doors, and as Wolfgang looked into it, he heard the door locks click.

Wolfgang pushed through. The room on the other side was massive, stretching fifty yards on either side before terminating against concrete walls. Dim lights shone from overhead, and pipes and electrical wires spider-webbed along the walls and through overhead latticeworks of metal.

The middle of the room was filled with row after open row of electrical cabinets with glass faces— probably some kind of complex audio or computer equipment now abandoned by the passage of time. The cabinets were dark and cast long shadows down a middle aisle that ran all the way to the back wall of the basement. Against that wall sat the HVAC units —massive metal beasts towering over the floor with air ducts shooting out from their sides and tops and running into the concert hall.

And standing in the middle of those HVAC units, wearing a gas mask, was Nigel.

11

Behind the full-face mask, Wolfgang saw Nigel's tight lips twist into a smile. They both broke into a run, Wolfgang unconsciously reaching for where his Beretta should be. He made it only two strides before a metal pipe rocketed out of the darkness and collided with his shoulder. Wolfgang went down, landing on his back with a cry of pain as a tall man in a gas mask leaned over him and lifted the pipe.

Wolfgang rolled to his right as he heard Megan slide to a stop. The pipe collided with the concrete, and Wolfgang motioned Megan on. "Go! Get Nigel!"

The next blow crashed into Wolfgang's ribs, and pain exploded through his body. He kicked out with both feet, landing blows on the man's shins and driving him backward. Every breath sent agony through Wolfgang's chest as he hauled himself to his feet. The pipe clattered to the concrete as the man crashed into one of the electrical cabinets, but before Wolfgang could reach for the pipe, the man hurled himself forward, and they both hit the floor.

Blows rained down across Wolfgang's face, and a knee landed in his stomach. He coughed and twisted, attempting to throw the man off, but he fought like a rabid jungle cat, striking with all four limbs while remaining on top of Wolfgang.

Megan. Nigel. The weapon.

Wolfgang reached down deep inside and found some rage—enough to twist his body like a catapult and sling the man into another cabinet. Glass shattered and rained over the floor. The man fell, and his mask busted against the concrete. He groaned and twisted, slinging the mask off.

Wolfgang scrambled backward and grabbed the pipe. The man stood up and spat blood, then turned, light spilling across his face. Wolfgang's breath caught in his throat. He'd seen this man before, in Rio. He was one of the kidnappers—the man Wolfgang confronted in front of the house. The man Wolfgang had wanted to kill but refused to do so.

"Wishing you'd killed me?" the man said, grinning. Blood glistened in his teeth from a busted lip, matching a deranged look in his eyes that chilled Wolfgang to the bone. "Hindsight's a bitch, ain't it?"

Wolfgang gritted his teeth and raised the pipe.

"Live and learn, bastard." He hurled himself forward, swinging for the man's head as if it were a baseball. The pipe collided with a defensive forearm, and bone snapped like a gunshot. Wolfgang's momentum carried him forward, and once again they crashed to the floor, but this time Wolfgang landed on top, and he wasn't letting go of the pipe.

The man reached for Wolfgang's throat with his good arm, and Wolfgang drove the end of the pipe straight into his mouth. Metal tore through flesh and knocked aside teeth, driving straight over his tongue and into his throat. The man thrashed, clawing at the pipe to dislodge it, but Wolfgang grabbed it with both hands and shoved down with his full bodyweight, driving the pipe straight through the man's neck.

Vertebrae collapsed, and the man fell limp, his eyes turning off as if he'd been unplugged. Wolfgang jerked the pipe out and checked quickly for a pistol but found only empty pockets.

A scream ripped from the back corner of the basement, followed by a suppressed gunshot. Wolfgang grabbed the pipe and ran, circling between storage cabinets and electrical boxes. The basement filled with the hum of the air conditioners, interrupted at random by the crash of metal and glass.

Wolfgang hurled himself down a last stretch of corridor between electrical cabinets. His feet crunched on shattered glass as he reached the back of the room, and he almost tripped on a fallen gas mask.

He didn't see Megan, but he heard another gunshot to his left. As he turned, his gaze crossed over air conditioners lining the back wall of the basement, standing twenty feet tall with a catwalk running along their tops. They hummed mechanically, filling the room with a growing din.

And then he saw it. The device on the catwalk was situated in the middle of the row of air conditioners. It was five feet long, constructed out of two metal bottles with hoses running from their tops and into a metal box mounted beneath them. From that box, another series of hoses ran out and split in different directions, each finding their way into an air duct.

But what caught his attention was the LCD display on the face of the box. A wave of dread mixed with déjà vu washed over him as he recognized the red outlines of numbers on the LCD, counting down from two minutes.

Another gunshot snapped to his left, lost in the shadows of the massive basement. Megan screamed, and Wolfgang lifted the pipe, a moment of confliction crossing through his mind as the image of the timer was overwhelmed by the pain of her cry.

I've got two minutes.

Wolfgang turned toward the direction of Megan's last scream, but before he could move, another pipe hissed through the air and glanced off the cabinet next to his ear. A third, smaller man lunged out of the darkness, slamming into him before he could move. Wolfgang landed on his back, and the pipe slipped out of his hand. Glass dug into his back, and he thrashed to the left, striking out with both hands. The man wore wire-rimmed glasses behind another full-face gas mask.

Pascha Koslov.

Wolfgang twisted to throw him off, but Koslov was too quick. He abandoned his pipe and reached straight for Wolfgang's throat. Crushing pressure enveloped his windpipe, cutting off air in an instant as Koslov bore down. His eyes were alight with the same bloodlust as the first man's, but the savageness in his attack defied basic physics.

Wolfgang clawed at his hands, twisted, and desperately tried to throw him off. Koslov clung on, and seconds stretched out in slow motion. From far above, Wolfgang heard the melodic blast of the Sydney Opera House's massive organ calling the guests into the main concert hall. From much closer, across the basement, he heard another crash and a scream. A man's scream. Maybe Nigel's.

And from directly on top of him, Koslov clamped down with both hands. The space around Koslov's head faded. Wolfgang's desperate attempts to dislodge him weakened, and his heart slowed. His fingers shook, and he continued to thrash, but still, Koslov clung on.

Overwhelming weight crushed down. Blackness closed in. The organ moaned from far above. Then the concrete shook, and a crashing sound boomed through the room, followed by another, and then a third. Koslov looked up, momentarily distracted as a fourth boom shook the concrete, then a fifth.

Wolfgang forced his head toward the noise. Electrical cabinets fell like dominos, knocking each other over one at a time. As each one hit the floor, the next toppled, and the basement filled with a shriek of metal on metal.

Koslov's fingers relaxed, and Wolfgang jerked his head to the side, dislodging the grip. Air surged into his windpipe, and Wolfgang struck out with his right hand, driving his fist into Koslov's windpipe. The Russian choked and let go of Wolfgang's throat. Wolfgang dropped his hand and fished for one of the fallen pipes, snatching one up and swinging full force at Koslov's head.

Koslov threw an arm up and blocked the blow. It glanced off his forearm, but Wolfgang followed it up with a jerking twist of his hips, slinging him to the ground. Again, glass bit into Wolfgang's back, and when he rolled to his knees, he saw Megan scrambling over the tops of fallen cabinets, blood streaming down her left arm. She shot him a glance.

"Get the weapon!" he yelled.

The words barely left his throat before a kick landed in his ribs. Pain ripped through his torso, blinding him for a moment as he fell and slammed his head against the concrete. The world spun, but his fingers touched the end of the fallen pipe. He grabbed it and swung blindly upward, clipping Koslov across the knee. The Russian stumbled back, and Wolfgang rolled to his knees, following the blow with a strike to the groin and then a slash across the stomach. Koslov doubled over and screamed.

Wolfgang staggered to his knees. His oxygen-deprived brain still wasn't ready to power his body, and no matter how much he wanted to dash forward to finish the job, he just couldn't.

Koslov looked up, and Wolfgang saw confusion and sadness in his face—the reality of a man lured into darkness, sickened by lies.

"You killed Katya," Koslov snarled.

He reached down for the second pipe, but Wolfgang didn't give him the chance. His brain finally cleared, and Wolfgang dashed forward, swinging down with the pipe as if it were an ax. It fell across Koslov's head with a brutal crunching of bone, and the Russian collapsed. The pipe fell from Wolfgang's hands, and he caught himself on the edge of a cabinet, almost tripping over the body at his feet.

Another gunshot.

Wolfgang ratcheted around, his feet catching on the dead man's legs as he searched for the source of the noise. The weapon sat on the catwalk, the timer counting down the last fifteen seconds before deadly gas would burst into the air ducts. Megan was halfway up the ladder to the catwalk, dragging herself along with one arm as the other hung uselessly at her side.

And Nigel stood thirty feet away amid the wreckage of fallen cabinets, his face a mess of blood and bruises, a pistol held in one shaking hand.

"No!" Wolfgang yelled. He jerked his leg free and threw himself forward, covering the last of the open space before he collided with a fallen cabinet. Sparks jumped at random from torn wires. Wolfgang hurtled over the top of the first cabinet as another gunshot cracked, and a bullet pinged off metal. Nigel staggered back, the gun swaying in his hand.

He stood twenty feet away, with four toppled cabinets between them. Nigel saw Wolfgang coming, but he didn't redirect the pistol. He fired again at the catwalk, and Wolfgang heard Megan bite back a scream. He fought his way over another cabinet and looked up to see her crawling along the catwalk, blood streaming from her hip, only ten feet away from the weapon. The timer read eight seconds, and Wolfgang hurled himself across the final two cabinets.

Nigel fired his last shot only a moment before Wolfgang hit him. They crashed to the floor amid the tangle of metal and wires, and the gun spun out of sight into the shadows. Wolfgang landed on top and drove his fist into Nigel's face.

Blood sprayed across Wolfgang's stomach, and Nigel tried to hit him, but whatever Megan had done to him had already weakened Nigel to the point of ineptitude. Wolfgang pounded his face again, driving his head into the concrete, then he wrapped his hands around Nigel's throat and squeezed. Wolfgang's shoulder's shook and his head swam so badly he almost fell over, but he didn't let go. He looked down into the pale, bloody face of SPIRE's right-hand man and pressed until Nigel's windpipe collapsed, then he grabbed him by the head and twisted as hard as he could.

Nigel's neck snapped, and his body lay still. Wolfgang sat astride him, gasping for air. He clawed his way off the body and turned back to the catwalk. The weapon lay in place, the LCD frozen in time at the two-second mark, and just next to it, Megan lay face-down, blood dripping from the underside of the catwalk.

"Megan!" Wolfgang screamed. He crashed through the cabinets again, heedless of the metal that tore through his hands and ripped into his legs, screaming her name the entire way. Megan didn't move or look up, and Wolfgang finally reached the bottom of the ladder and hauled himself up.

Every breath felt like a shotgun blast to his ribs, and he couldn't see straight. His hands kept slipping from the rungs of the ladder, and twice he almost fell, catching himself at the last second. At last, he reached the top of the ladder and clawed his way across the metal mesh. Everything was slick with

Megan's blood, and as he continued to call her name, she still didn't move.

"Megan!"

As he drew closer, Wolfgang saw her left hand extended toward the weapon, a fistful of ripped-off wires tangled around her fingers. He reached her and tore his jacket off, pressing it against the bullet wound in her hip. A second wound oozed blood from her shoulder, and when he rolled her over, he saw the third wound—Nigel's last shot. It hit her in the stomach, just below the ribcage, and shot upward into her chest cavity. Wolfgang didn't see an exit wound, and as he laid her down on her back, Megan's eyes didn't open. Her chest didn't move. He clawed away the sleeve of her jacket and felt for a pulse, but his hands shook too hard to feel anything.

"Megan!" he cried. Tears slipped down his cheeks, and he leaned over her, pumping on her chest and breathing into her mouth. Her stomach was soggy with blood, and her face smeared with it. He pushed frantically, counting between pumps, and then stopped to force air into her lungs.

Megan's eyes fluttered. Wolfgang felt a surge of hope, and he pumped again, leaning down and blowing more air into her mouth. As he went to pump the third time, Megan slowly blinked, and her lips parted.

"Megan!" he said again, grabbing her hand. "I'm here! You're going to be okay. Stay with me!"

Megan's mouth lifted into the softest, weakest of smiles, and he felt her fingers wrap around his.

"Hold on," he said, gripping her hand. "I'm going to get you out of here."

Meagan tried to lift her head.

"Stay still, baby," he said. "Everything's going to be okay."

Again, her lips parted, and he thought he heard a word. He pressed his ear close to her mouth and felt her hand tighten around his.

"Tell it to the ring," she whispered.

Then her head fell back against the catwalk, and her grip loosened.

Wolfgang's heart pounded, and he sat up, squeezing her hand, and again, checking for a pulse. But there was nothing.

"Megan . . . baby," he whispered. "Don't go."

But Megan lay still, her eyes closed, and that faint smile forever frozen on her lips.

12

R ed lights flashed from two dozen emergency vehicles around the Sydney Opera House, and helicopters surged overhead. People screamed, and men in suits ran around shouting. The Australian Defence Force showed up with a chemical and biological weapons unit to sweep the facility. Dignitaries were evacuated. Checkpoints were established. Patrol boats roared through Sydney Harbor.

Basically, everything was done that would've been really helpful two hours earlier, but none of it mattered because the weapon had already been disabled and the terrorists neutralized.

And Megan ripped away.

Wolfgang sat in an interrogation room at a government building in downtown Sydney, his hands cuffed to the tabletop, hasty bandages applied to his numerous wounds. Some of his ribs were broken, glass cuts covered his back, arms, and legs, and his hair was caked with blood.

He didn't care. He didn't care that he was hand-cuffed to the tabletop or that he was beaten to pieces. He didn't care that the Australians thought he was a terrorist or that the world outside was descending into chaos despite being saved from annihilation.

He just felt numb and empty. It was a familiar feeling—a feeling of loss he first encountered as a child when his mother and best friend were murdered. The cavern left by those losses was immense, but this was worse. It tore down to the very foundations of everything he was and ripped away the very meaning of life. It left him something less than a shell, with no idea which way was up or what the meaning of his next breath was. It left him medically alive, but by all other measures, as lifeless as Megan.

The door to the interrogation room rattled, and Wolfgang looked up. His vision was blurred by tears that had long since dried. He stared at the solid steel door and flinched when something like a battering ram slammed against it.

Then he heard Ivan's voice, low and brutally cold. "You will let me in, little man, or I will crush your skull like beer can."

There was a choking, gurgling sound, followed by the buzz and click of the electric lock. The door burst open, and Ivan Sidorov stepped in. His tie was gone, and his hair and jacket were disheveled. Deep strain covered his face like Wolfgang hadn't seen before.

Ivan shut the door and stood for a long moment, staring at Wolfgang. He scraped a chair backward and sat down, leaning back with one giant hand resting on the table. "You were right, Amerikos."

Wolfgang didn't answer.

"You save many lives tonight," Ivan said. "You save . . . the world."

To Wolfgang, the concept of saving the world was such a trite, obscure thing, like ending hunger or developing renewable energy—something that had a definition but was impossible to picture or really understand. Hearing the words meant nothing to him. They failed to breach the fog around his head or assign meaning to anything that had just happened.

"Koslov was there," Wolfgang said. "I killed him."

"Da. The Australians have the body."

"So that's it, then. It's over." His words sounded empty, even to him.

Ivan sighed. "With these people, it is never over. As long as they breathe, they will try again. But this is not for you to worry about. I will crush them."

Wolfgang heard the words, but he didn't really process them.

Ivan leaned forward. "Amerikos . . . You are hero."

Wolfgang couldn't hold it back anymore. He crumpled forward, and when he spoke, his voice cracked. "She's gone."

Ivan sat still for a while, and then to Wolfgang's surprise, he placed one rough hand on Wolfgang's arm and gave it a powerful squeeze. "She is hero, also," he said. "And in your heart, she lives forever."

————

Ivan influenced—or perhaps threatened—the Australians into releasing Wolfgang, and he was taken into Russian custody. A Mercedes SUV appeared and drove them across town to Ivan's hotel, where an army of Russians were busy shouting at each other and making phone calls. Lyle was there, and he threw himself at Wolfgang, wrapping him in a tight hug as soon as they walked in. Lyle hung on for a long time, and when he finally let go, his smudged glasses were fogged and wet.

Ivan led them into an adjoining room and closed the door. The Russian poured himself a generous portion of vodka from the minibar and took a long sip, then turned to Wolfgang. "We have a plane ready. You are guest of Russian government for as long as you wish."

"You're taking us to Russia?" Lyle asked.

Ivan shrugged. "I take you wherever you want to go. You are not prisoners."

Wolfgang stared out the open hotel window. Their suite was on the twentieth floor of the hotel, and he could clearly see the flash of red lights reflecting into the night sky from the opera house. The military had closed off that entire section of the city, but news vans clustered around the barriers, and people crowded in for a look.

Nobody was actually afraid, he realized. Nobody really appreciated how close their entire planet had come to toppling into endless chaos. These people were so sheltered behind their established systems of peace and prosperity that everything happening at the opera house was more fascinating than terrifying.

They have no idea. And they never will.

Ivan stepped to the window next to Wolfgang, and they watched the emergency lights together in silence. The dog and pony show would go on for weeks, maybe months. Presidents would make declarations. Congress would hold hearings. New laws would pass, and global task forces would be formed. All those useless things that failed to appreciate the point: lives were saved because Megan saved them. It was as simple as that.

"Can I ask a favor?" Wolfgang asked.

"Anything," Ivan said.

"Can you get her body, please?"

Ivan sipped his vodka. "I will make some calls. Anything else?"

Wolfgang shook his head. "Just take me home."

EPILOGUE

Four Months Later

Summer came to Upstate New York in a gentle wave, bringing the forest to life with a thousand songbirds and a dozen shades of green. A warm breeze blew between the hardwoods, bringing with it the smell of blooming flowers and the brook that ran along the east edge of the property.

Wolfgang walked along a trail that wound between the trees and thickets, cradling a bouquet of fresh-cut roses in one arm and breathing in the peace of the forest around him. It was a clear day, and the temperature was perfect—warm enough to drive out the chills of an endless winter, but cool enough to bask in the sun without sweating.

It was exactly the kind of day he always dreamed of sharing with Megan.

Wolfgang stooped on the trail to pick up a fallen limb, then tossed it into a thicket and watched as a rabbit jumped out. It hopped onto the trail and sat for a moment, watching him out of one beady black eye. He stood still and cradled the roses, waiting until the rabbit bounded back into the forest amid a flurry of fallen leaves. Then Wolfgang started off down the trail again, picking his way around a rotting log and eventually arriving at the meadow.

Golden sun bathed the clearing in warmth, while a gentle breeze rustled the leaves of a few dozen wild sunflowers that grew amid the tall grass. Wolfgang stopped to admire the beauty, then looked up at the sky, enjoying the warmth on his face.

A perfect day to remember.

The first of the graves lay just outside the tree line, marked by a simple granite stone with a name and a death date, but no birthdate. Wolfgang wasn't sure when Kevin was born, but the director had contacted the Army, and he'd add the birthdate when they got back to him. A dead stick had fallen on the grave, and Wolfgang tossed it into the trees before moving to the next headstone.

Edric's grave was identical to Kevin's, but it featured a birthdate, along with a simple epitaph carved in elegant script.

Loyal friend. Fearless leader. Loving father.

Wolfgang dusted the top of the stone and took a moment to read the epitaph to himself. It had taken him almost two days to decide on the right words, and he still wasn't sure they were perfect. Edric was all of those things and none of those things at the same time. He was Wolfgang's friend, yet he was also his boss. He was a leader, yet he often accepted guidance from his team. He was a father, even though he had no children.

Wolfgang smiled and rubbed the headstone with one thumb, then continued to the last grave.

Megan's headstone was different than the rest. It was large, with ornate scrolling on the edges and an engraved image of Tokyo Tower carved into the bottom right-hand corner. Her name was written in deep, elegant script, with her birthdate and death date carved beneath.

No epitaph graced the stone. He wanted there to be one, and someday there would be, but the words just wouldn't come. How would he describe a person who was everything to him? Somebody who made the world spin, who brought color to the sky, who made him laugh and cry and want to scream all in the same day?

Wolfgang lifted the roses out of his arm and gently set them at the base of the stone. It still hurt to bend, or to twist, or to move in general. His ribs were almost healed, but if he breathed deeply enough, the pain was there. Given long enough, those aches would probably fade, but the emptiness he felt never would. There would always be a chasm inside where Megan's heart had belonged.

Always.

Wolfgang took a moment to stand with Megan's stone and think about Tokyo and Miami and all the moments in between. He whispered a few loving words, just in case she was someplace nearby and could hear. Wolfgang wasn't sure what lay on the other side of death or where lost souls found rest, but he liked to believe Megan was closer to him than he was to her. He liked to believe she heard his soft words of affection and that it brightened her day on the other side.

Wolfgang slipped a hand between the buttons of his shirt and felt Megan's engagement ring hanging around his neck. He remembered her last words and then closed his eyes to keep from crying. It felt wrong to cry on a day like this. It was too bright and beautiful.

"Happy Monday," he whispered. "I love you."

He knelt at the edge of the grave and readjusted the roses before putting his hands in his pockets and starting back down the trail, through the trees, to where his rental car waited next to the road. The property still didn't have a driveway or a proper address. It sat by itself on a lonely country road, the future home of a family that would never be. Wolfgang thought he might build on it someday. Maybe clear out a space in the trees and build a house or cabin. He knew he wanted to live there . . . eventually. For now, he just wanted to know it was there—to know Megan was there—and that he could be with her whenever he wanted.

He rolled the windows down and enjoyed the summer breeze during the half-hour drive to Buffalo. On the way, he stopped and purchased some candy and an oversized stuffed pink bear with a big smile on its face. The bear rode beside him the last five miles to Jordan Fletcher Home for Children, and then he carried it in, along with the candy, waving to the receptionist on his way to the elevator.

"Good morning, Mr. Ward!"

Inside the elevator, gentle music played, probably designed to amplify the calming, peaceful atmosphere the home was designed to create. Jordan Fletcher was the best, after all, with no expense spared. It was paid for by the generous, anonymous donations of people around the world. Lately, there had been several substantial donations from a now-defunct espionage company out of St. Louis, and even an anonymous contribution from somebody in Russia.

Collins's well-being was funded for the foresee-able future, but eventually, that money would run out. Wolfgang would need to figure out a way to pay the bills and keep her safe and happy. He wondered if there was some kind of advanced medical treat-ments she could benefit from. Maybe research into her disease could be accelerated, given the right amount of funding.

He'd have to look into that.

The elevator stopped, and Wolfgang stepped out, drawing in a deep breath. He stared at the bear and thought about his little sister and how many years it had been since he'd seen her. He thought about the guilt he bore for all those years of cowardice. All the pain that had kept them apart.

And then he just shelved all of that. Because life was brutally short, and he wasn't going to leave things unsaid anymore.

Wolfgang put a hand on Collins's door and eased it open. Cartoons played on the other side, and the hiss of Collins's oxygen bottle pumped vital support into her lungs.

"Collins?" he said.

"Ricky?"

AFTERWORD

When Wolfgang first stepped onto the page in *Hunt to Kill*, the second book in my Reed Montgomery series, I had no idea how much I would come to love the character or how far his story would develop.

Wolfgang was originally the invention of my wife, Anna, who spotted a gentleman dressed in a plaid jacket at a graduation and said: "He looks cool. He should be in one of your books."

We spent the afternoon inventing a backstory for this man we'd never met, and Anna named him Wolfgang Pierce.

She's often told me (with no lack of irritation) that the Wolfgang Pierce who stormed the pages of the Reed Montgomery series is nothing like the character she invented, but I like my version. He's deep, and unique, and (I hope) a departure from the classic image of a brutal assassin.

I never intended to write a series for Wolfgang, but my readers had other feelings. He quickly became a fan favorite, particularly of two very special Reed Montgomery fans, Abby and Naomi.

They're both passionate readers and have supported my work from the start, helping me to keep writing long before anybody bought my books or wrote me emails about Reed and Wolfgang.

So it made sense to me when I gave Wolfgang his own series that Abby and Naomi should be involved. I texted them one day and asked them to name six international cities they'd love to read a story set in. I didn't share details of my project, or even tell them it involved Wolfgang. We just spent the afternoon talking about exciting, exotic locales, and eventually landed on the six cities which would hallmark this series: Paris, Cairo, Moscow, Rio, Tokyo, and Sydney.

Six months later I typed the last words of *That Time in Sydney*.

I originally hoped for this series to bridge the gap between Wolfgang's early years and his life as a professional assassin—The Wolf. As you can tell, I only covered about half that ground, ending his story in summer of 2012, about six years before Wolfgang meets Reed.

I may return to fill that gap with further novels, but for now, I'll leave it to your imagination.

I want to thank my wife, Anna, for first sparking my imagination and giving me the idea for Wolfgang.

I know he's nothing like you dreamed, but maybe one day you'll forgive me.

I want to thank Abby and Naomi, my original superfans, for years of relentless support, encouragement, and kindness. You guys really are the coolest, and I'm so grateful for the part you've played in these stories.

I want to thank my editor, Sarah Flores, for her continued support and hard work on all my stories, and especially these. I'm sorry I work you so hard, but I can't imagine crafting this series without your help.

I want to thank my entire Advance Team for their incredible support during the launch phase of this series, and for all the encouragement, feedback, and kind reviews. I seriously couldn't do my job without you guys.

And finally, to the people who inspired Megan, Lyle, Kevin, and Edric . . .

You don't know who you are, but I'll always be grateful for the roles you've played in my story.

All my best,
Logan

ABOUT THE AUTHOR

Logan Ryles is the author of the Reed Montgomery thriller series, and the Wolfgang Pierce espionage series. You can learn more about Logan's books, sign up for email updates, and connect with him directly by visiting LoganRyles.com.

ALSO BY LOGAN RYLES

THE WOLFGANG PIERCE SERIES

Prequel: *That Time in Appalachia* (read for free at LoganRyles.com)

Book 1: *That Time in Paris*

Book 2: *That Time in Cairo*

Book 3: *That Time in Moscow*

Book 4: *That Time in Rio*

Book 5: *That Time in Tokyo*

Book 6: *That Time in Sydney*

THE REED MONTGOMERY SERIES

Prequel: *Sandbox*, a short story (read for free at LoganRyles.com)

Book 1: *Overwatch*

Book 2: *Hunt to Kill*

Book 3: *Total War*

Book 4: *Smoke and Mirrors*

Book 5: *Survivor*

Book 6: *Death Cycle*

Book 7: *Sundown*

LoganRyles.com

Printed in Great Britain
by Amazon

82637369R00082